LORENZ TRAVELING DIARIES -
THE RISE OF DAVIAN

A NOVELLA BY
DRAEGON GREY

Published by: FST PULP
First Printing: May 2014
Story by: Draegon Grey
Edited by: Angela Thang

ISBN: 978-1-935582-33-5

info@fstpulp.com

Dedication
This is dedicated to all the readers that enjoyed traveling in my world. There are many more adventures to come.

Enjoy the ride!

ACKNOWLEDGMENTS:

My endless thanks go to:

The many family members and friends who continue to support me.

My Mother.

And Daniel, who works tirelessly to support and help FST PULP to grow.

TABLE OF CONTENTS

PREFACE

Lorenz continues his adventure. Having survived his first few harrowing battles, he and the dwarves team up with an Elvisan comrade to search for his captive brother. Meanwhile, a relentless police sheriff is on the hunt for Lorenz, on account of murder.

In a race against time, they must find the prisoner soon if they are to save his life... and beat Davian to the secret cave of dragons.

CHAPTER ONE: THE EMERGENCE OF CIGAM

There was a time during the second epoch, when peace and prosperity existed throughout the lands. An incredible force, cigam, had become a major part of society. It was a source of energy that—combined with nature—could heal wounds and illness and helped to create a world of harmony. Cigam had always existed, yet few knew of it. Even fewer could use it, much less master it. Some feared the power as unholy or unnatural, but once in the right hands, cigam brought forth an age of serenity at a time when all the living beings of the world had been at desperate odds with one another.

A well-intentioned group of cigamians worked tirelessly to this end. They would be there to right wrongs—rejuvenating the sick, composing the disturbed of heart, mending the broken, and bringing balance back. People were able to rest easy once again, knowing that there were others out there to help them.

Those who learned cigam were individuals of many races and origins throughout the globe. The many cigamians spent countless hours studying and learning all they could to properly wield the power. When they were called upon in times of need, they did not hesitate to respond. They understood that their abilities were important in their communities and accepted the burden of their skills. The users of cigam often believed it was their purpose in life to assist those who needed their help. From aiding the infirm to defending the towns from wild beasts, the cigamians toiled in their research, discovering ever more spells.

As these people delved deeper into the practice of cigam, its uses and purposes expanded. Its effect increased not only on mankind, but upon beasts and objects as well. Those who became very skilled with cigam eventually learned how to transfer some of its power to objects. A stick became a wand, a mere hat could be worn as a helmet, and plain water and leaves could make a potent healing salve. This further elevated the significance of the cigamians within their communities. Not only did they provide useful tools for work and medicine, their cigam-imbued products could be sold or traded to other towns and villages, which caused a boom in those local economies that were lucky enough to have such talented cigmanians.

As the ability to use cigam became a highly prized skill, non-cigamians who wanted to get in on the rewards quickly found that despite their effort, not just anyone could master it. Cigam itself almost seemed to choose who could wield its power and the energies would thus resonate favorably within certain folk. Over generations, the select few users grew into many who grew up to learn the ways of cigam. Family traditions began to emerge. Children born into families of cigamians would begin their training early on, some gradually mastering the skill and the others failing to move beyond the basics.

In the end, many were destined to become adept cigamians. Unfortunately, with so many people across the globe joining the ranks of the cigamians, the abuse of cigam's power was inevitable. Gifted users were loved and respected and they quickly gained political and social prominence within their communities. Desirous of greater wealth or glory, it wasn't long before a few cigamians started to use their powers more for personal gain. They believed that they deserved more, and so twisting the minds of the weak-willed and cutting deals with thugs and gangs, the shrewder ones who abused cigam's energies were able to become powerful beyond belief.

CHAPTER TWO: SMALL BEGINNINGS

Davian had not been born the feared cigamian warlord he was known as now; he had once been a scrawny little boy once with a mop of messy dark hair, growing up in a tiny island village in the boonies. Often feeling estranged and lonely in the sleepy little town, he spent his days studying for the most part and received top marks in primary school. As a child born to a wealthy cigamian family, many of the older kids whispered rumors or picked on him, but he soon learned to put them in their place with his quick wit... and a little bit of his gift.

Thanks to the bothersome, thick-headed children of town, Davian learned early on that he had a knack at manipulating others. Before they knew it, Davian's childhood bullies were bowing down to him as a great sage and their best friend before it was said and done, bringing him gifts, escorting him around town, carrying his books and whatever else. They never even saw it coming; as the best cigam using kid in the whole island, following him just felt natural. Planting his invisible seeds in their minds, Davian ensured that they would believe this. Even as a toddler, all he needed to do was force a cloying smile and laugh and he would have all the adults eating out of his hands. It appeared everyone was under his spell.

As he entered secondary school in his teens, his mental prowess only continued to grow in leaps and bounds. He excelled in math and science, subjects particularly useful in using cigam. There were times when even the teachers would ask him for his opinions during their lectures, granting opportunities aplenty to demonstrate his vast knowledge. Even at his young age, he shortly served as a lecturer on the school grounds. Needless to say, his parents were very proud of his accomplishments.

His father in particular realized that Davian would become a powerful man someday. Naturally, like any father would, he encouraged his son to love his family, respect his elders and to never forget where he came from. The older man was no fool. He could see how his son took advantage of the other village kids, talking them into giving away their candy or lunch money. He feared that if his young son was using his abilities for underhanded tricks now, what Davian might grow up to do when he was older.

"You're a smart boy, Davian," his father said. "I'm real proud of you, son. Your mother and I love you more than anything in the world. We want nothing more than for you to be happy and to always use your talents to help people."

Davian's reply to his father when he was talking like this was always, "I know, Dad."

It seemed like his father was giving him these talks more and more as he got older. It had started being tiresome to listen to even years ago as a small child. It almost seemed as if his father were *afraid* of him. Like he would do something bad with his powers.

"It's not like I'm doing anything bad," Davian thought to himself. "My father is just jealous of me being smarter, because I'm already more powerful than he could ever be in ten lifetimes."

And though he did not voice his true feelings to his mother or father, this was the lingering sentiment in Davian's heart for the years as he grew up.

CHAPTER THREE: THE CREATOR'S WORK

For a long time, there lived an extremely powerful being who reigned supreme over many worlds amongst several others of his kind. Together, they ruled over the many worlds of the universe in the same way, begetting the same results in the same fashion, always. The sun and planets and moon stood static and nothing but wind and dust blew across the wild landscapes of their realms. That is, until one decided that it was time to do things differently.

He created a new land out of the space he resided in and populated it with creatures of his own design. For centuries, the Creator watched as these little creatures lived together in harmony. These animals he called "dragons" blossomed routinely, having little ones growing in numbers. Still uninspired, they were all the same size and the same color: grey, just like the dusty stones they scampered across.

"Why don't I give them some more unique traits? Something to make them different?" he thought.

And so, he painted the different dragons of his many different colors. Red, green, blue, and violet—all the colors he enjoyed from the twinkling stars in the distant galaxies he watched.

In their shiny new scales, the dragons roamed about the earth aimlessly and after a short while, the creatures seemed to be unhappy. They lay across the bare dirt and panted sickly. That was then the Creator realized that his new creations were not as powerful as he was, and that he needed to provide the creatures with some form of sustenance.

With this in mind, he carved great lines and pits into the earth and they filled with cold clear water, which the animals immediately rushed towards to drink and bathe. But that wasn't enough, as they still looked ill, even after they had drank their fill. So, the Creator sprinkled something across the land and green began to sprout from the sterile earth everywhere. Vines and trees and shrubs erupted from the soil, flowers bloomed, fruits grew from them, and other animals soon followed.

The dragons now had other creatures and plants throughout the world to keep them company and to fill their hungry bellies. But they were still not content. One of the dragons dug at the stony ground, trying to build itself a little hollow to sleep in. So the Creator gave the one dragon in particular the ability to alter reality and manipulate its environment with its mind rather than just with its claws. This power was called cigam.

The power made the life of this particular dragon different. Very quickly, the beast learned to use its powers to excavate huge amounts of soil and build itself a hugely expansive cavern in the ground to live in. Rather than having to chew or paw at the ground like the other base animals, the dragon was able to force away the dirt with mere breaths and swipes of its claws.

Naturally, this dragon had a significant advantage over the others. It was faster and stronger, and therefore soon took more territory and more food from the others, and hoarded the meats and fruits in his large cave den. Noting this disparity, the Creator decided to give all the dragons the power to use cigam in order to recreate balance within the species.

The cigam took to the different dragons in different ways, causing various effects aside from increasing their overall strength. It made the red dragons breathe fire. A green dragon would breathe an airborne noxious gas. Blue dragons would breathe a liquid that underwent an endothermic reaction and caused freezing temperature. Lastly, a violet dragon would secrete an acutely paralyzing poison.

Once he finished creating these enormously powerful creatures, the Creator realized that he should create an all-powerful dragon that could destroy the lesser dragons if they were to ever get out of control. With this in mind, he created a massive five-headed dragon of five colors. Each head of this dragon had the same abilities as the lesser ones and was impervious to their powers. The great beast would be hidden away, only to emerge if the other dragons of the world grew out of control.

He placed this grand dragon and gathered most of the lesser dragons into a cave deep below the surface of the earth, in an expansive cavern where they rested and fed in peace. There, they could reign with the subterranean expanses as their domain. Clear water flowed through underground rivers for the beasts to bathe and drink, and carried with it small fish and shrimp and vegetation. With all the food and water they needed, there was never any need for the dragons to come back to the surface. However, anticipating that the dragons might gradually become weary of their tedious living situation, the Creator placed carefully hidden mounds gold, silver, and other shining precious metals and stones for them to dig up and find. Over time, the great dragon and his cohorts discovered and amassed an incredible amount of glittering riches, piling them high in his den, where they glinted softly under the gentle glow of luminescent crystals and fungus.

The Creator had put away his beautiful creations because he had decided to make a few more additions that he wanted to live upon the world surface under the protective warmth and splendor of the sun. The dragons were strong enough to live on their own in the cold and darkness of the caverns, and they were too powerful to allow to roam the earth freely; they would conquer the landscape if left unchecked and the Creator wanted to bring more interesting creatures into the world—not just dragons and their feed.

He made other incredible animals and plants and amazing creatures of all sorts—beasts with long noses like living rope, others with necks as tall as the trees, swimming animals and trees as large as small mountains—but he wasn't yet done. It felt incomplete. Despite the splendor of his populated planet, there was a certain quality that the living things all lacked. Finally, he realized that he should make inhabitants that possessed the ability to plan and think on their own, like him.

The Creator put all of his ingenuity into designing this last creature. Though the newest creations were made intelligent, he made them smaller and weaker of body to counterbalance their strength of wit. He could feel that he was nearly complete, but needed to ensure that the new beings would be safe in the world that he created. Therefore, he gave some of them the ability to use cigam and then finally rested his hands.

The new young men and women he crafted seemed to be perfect. They used their minds to solve problems and words to communicate ideas. Their hands were put to use to tame the wilds around them, to farm food and build warm, comfortable homes.

For eons, the world took its natural course, all elements in equilibrium. Life followed death, day replaced night. His creatures grew and changed and the peoples below continuously bettered themselves and built cities and legacies despite many difficulties. Illness, famine, inclement weather—the peoples below were learning and developing better tools to overcome these things and uncovering better techniques to use their cigam every day. The Creator was proud of his work and watched them all with joy in his heart.

Things remained prosperous and peaceful for many generations. Feeling at last satisfied, the Creator vowed to never again directly involve himself in the lives and happenings of his creations and allowed them to continue to conduct lives of their own.

CHAPTER FOUR: FORBIDDEN BEASTS

One bright and sunny afternoon, the great oval sun was high in the sky. Young Davian was coming home from a long day of studying at the library after school while walking down the path headed toward his home on the outskirts of town. The town library was next to his school which was located on a hill about a half mile from the main road, a fair walk in the nearly summer heat. The path was lined with tall lush walnut trees which blocked the hot sunlight from the travelers walking below their branches.

Davian walked alone today, deep in thought. As he trod along the path quietly by himself, the sunlight danced along his face in dappled bursts of brightness and darkness, and as he turned out of the tree line, the light beamed down directly onto his face.

Davian looked upwards, shielding his eyes from the intense rays with his hand. Feeling the incredible warmth against his hands, a thought floated through his mind:

"I wonder what it would be like to have the power of the sun."

While at the library earlier, he had dug out some dusty tomes from one of the back shelves and read them in curiosity. They were so coated in grimy dust and cobwebs in their sad little corner at the foot of the back bookshelf, Davian estimated that they must not have been read in decades. Most of the older-looking books were about the ancient and mythological beasts of the world. After spending hours poring through these tomes, one animal kept coming to mind.

He continued pondering, "What if I could control one of those creatures? Those *dragons*."

He had heard the term "dragon" here and there a few times before, but never knew what they were, so he had never spent the time to think about them before. From what he could gather from the old texts, they were cigam-using beasts of immense power that had either been all destroyed or sealed away.

"One day, I am going to be as powerful as the sun," Davian swore. "Everyone will respect me and look to me for everything, just how the leaves and flowers follow the sun each day."

He needed to ask someone to tell him more about the dragons, information that he couldn't find written down in any book. He'd done enough research to have a gut feeling that they weren't just a mere myth.

Davian approached his home, a large four-story red and brown brick building surrounded by vibrantly blooming brush and greenery. It was the largest and most beautiful home in town, thanks to the old money saved from generations of talented past cigamians in their family.

As he approached the front door, he shouted, "Dad! Where are you? I need to talk to you about something."

"Back here, son."

Davian, picked up the pace to father's location around back. He quickly reached his father whom he found on his knees, planting a root cutting of a redbud tree. Normally such a small cutting wouldn't be able to take root and grow, but with a little nudge from the cigam in his hands, the man was able to maintain the best-looking garden that anyone had ever seen.

Davian's father, Deacon, a broad man standing 5'11", was by all means a good-looking and very intelligent middle-aged man. He served as one of the town's council members and was well-loved in the community despite his somewhat conceited and antisocial son. Though now less agile and energetic than when he was younger, Deacon was in the backyard working up a sweat in the garden when he heard his son's call.

"What is it that you needed to ask me, boy?" he inquired softly.

"I want to hear more about those creatures that no one seems to know much about," Davian said frankly. "The dragons."

"The dragons...?" Deacon repeated, wiping his brow with the back of his hand, smearing dirt across his wet skin. "What are you talking about?" he continued while he continued to dig into the soil with a spade, feigning ignorance.

As an older and learned government official of the village, Deacon did in fact know about the existence of dragons. However, he had been getting more of a bad feeling about his son's growing powers. Davian only seemed interested in using his knowledge and powers to boss the other kids around and show off at school. That wasn't what cigam should be used for.

Davian had always had confidence in his abilities, which was good. Confidence in oneself was a healthy thing, but Davian took it much further than that. He had been becoming increasingly arrogant for many years, putting down his schoolmates and even teachers and adults, getting into pointless arguments, and manipulating the dimmer kids into becoming his personal escorts. Until Davian could demonstrate more maturity and selflessness, Deacon did not want his son to know anything about the dragons.

"If he finds out where the dragons are located, if he is able to get a dragon under his influence—his control... Who knows what might happen...?" Deacon thought worriedly to himself. He desperately hoped that Davian would soon forget about the dragons all together if he could throw him off the trail.

"Son, as you may remember me mentioning before, dragons are just these big mythical animals that are special because they possess special powers in the stories. Remember, the important thing about myths is that there is no proof that they really exist. They were most likely made up by people many millennia ago to pass the time or explain different phenomena in the world," Deacon explained calmly.

"I know, I know," said Davian impatiently. "I just want to hear about the dragons again—especially about their powers."

Deacon continued his story after raising himself from the ground and brushing the soil from his trousers. He looked Davian directly in his eyes and placed his hand on Davian's shoulder, guiding his son as they both headed to the oak bench that faced the garden. It was old, but comfortable and worn smooth from years of polishing and sitting to gaze upon the garden, his temple.

"As the tales go, the special powers the dragons possess can change many kinds of things. For example, it is said that they have the ability to change ordinary swords into incredible weapons of power. And that they can heal any creature to good health, even if ailing to the point of death. The myths say that they could even control the weather, causing lightning, floods, hail or earthquakes."

At the mention of lightning and earthquakes, Davian's eyes appeared to light up.

Seeing this, Deacon coolly added, "Son, I am sure that there is no power that exists that could create such destruction. After all, what good could come out of something like making earthquakes and floods?" reasoned Deacon.

"It just sounds pretty cool, Dad," replied Davian with a small smirk.

Deacon laughed lightly, hiding his nervousness. "You're getting to be a grown boy, Davian. A little too old for these old wives' tales, don't you think?" he asked gently.

"C'mon, Dad. I never ask you to tell me any stories, so just humor me this once," pled Davian with a playful tone, laying a hand on his father's arm.

"Oh, all right," Deacon complied uncomfortably, continuing the discussion against his better judgment. "According to the old myths, dragons love anything shiny, especially gold and silver and gems. They have amassed incredible amounts of this treasure in their dens. Also, they are incredibly dangerous. Some breathe fire or poison. They are territorial, aggressive creatures that don't get along with any other creatures or people. Naturally, the myths conclude with most, if not all, of the dragons dying out."

"None are—I mean—*would be* around today?"

"No, this is a land of people. Not monsters." Deacon's words were curt.

"Where did they live? I won't ask any more questions after this, Dad," begged the boy with his sweet child eyes.

"Well, big animals usually live in caves, right?" Deacon reasoned.

"Yes, but what caves, Dad? Caves like the ones where the old fishermen go to hunt for crayfish?"

Deacon sighed. "No, caves like the ones located on the other side of the Mountain Nemor," he blurted out without thinking. He wondered if Davian was influencing him to be this talkative about the topic that he'd originally felt so apprehensive about telling him about.

Davian only smiled at his father while Deacon's trepidation grew. It was too late to stop now. Deacon would just try to wrap it up quickly.

"But they say a huge lightning storm came and destroyed that face of the mountain and they all died," he declared.

"I don't believe that one storm could destroy an entire mountain and all the creatures in it," Davian pouted. "It doesn't make sense. It's impossible."

Deacon just shrugged. "That's what the story says, son. It's just a myth, after all. There have been no reports of dragons for ages, obviously. They only appear in old storybooks and all storybooks have an end."

"For my birthday, maybe I'll wish for a dragon to show up," joked Davian.

"Perhaps, if the Creator is willing." Deacon smiled at his son tiredly. "It's dinner time. Let's go inside."

"Okay!" Davian leapt spryly from his seat and headed towards the house.

As the two climbed up the stairs, Deacon placed his heavy hand on top of his son's head. He quickly ruffled Davian's messy black hair in a playful gesture and his son smiled back at him.

CHAPTER FIVE: HERE BE DRAGONS

Several years later, an older Davian in his late teens had gotten into the sport of spelunking in the caves about fifteen miles north of his hometown. Most of his free time was spent reading about science and nature, focusing particularly on prehistoric herpetology and geology. He usually explored at least a few miles deep into the mountain caves there and would be gone for days at a time. Becoming completely obsessed with the caves, he'd quit his teaching job in town and would hardly even talk to other townsfolk any more. He was always too busy with the caves.

This fateful day, Davian was in his bedroom studying as usual. His mother, even at her age still a stately beauty crowned with long raven locks, was putting on her coat and hat and preparing to go downtown to do errands at the local shops. She had to do the usual of picking up groceries, feed for the livestock, and now also medicine. Before leaving, however, she asked Davian if he would cut up some fresh fruit to bring to his father while she was gone, as her errands would take her several hours. Deacon was working in the backyard garden, where he had always loved to spend his time, and despite his wife's reminders, he often forgot to eat lunch while he busied himself outside.

In spite of his efforts, the garden was not as trimmed as it used to be. Deacon was getting older and had been in poor health recently. He could no longer upkeep the huge yard on his own. His once robust and stout body had wasted away and his ruddy skin was now sickly pallid. He had come down with an illness several months ago that caused his whole body to ache and he suffered from recurring fevers. Still, Deacon tried his best to clip branches, pull weeds and rake up leaves and debris.

Sighing with reluctance, Davian got out of his chair and headed downstairs to the kitchen where he quickly rinsed and sliced up a few apples and pears. He hated to be disturbed by his parents while reading, but he knew that his father was sick and needed the care.

He put the fruit onto a plate and carried it out impatiently to the garden. He walked quickly, wanting to get back to his reading as soon as he could, and accidentally bumped into their small fire pit in the backyard. The metal container fell noisily onto its side with a clatter, spilling black and white ashes and bits of burnt paper and spent charcoal all across the garden path. Davian noticed a larger scrap of parchment that still had a few legible words on it.

Deacon, still several feet away, rose to his feet immediately with a pained grunt. "Oh, Davian. Don't worry, boy. I'll clean that mess up. You can just go back to your studies. I can take it from here."

Ignoring him, Davian set the plate of food down on the ground and picked up the piece of paper and read it.

"-mastering the dragon is the power to control, to change and manipulate the physical world itself. One must use his cigam-" and it ended, lost in unforgiving black char. The rest had been forever burnt away. Again, he read the enigmatic words.

"What is this?" Davian demanded.

He did not bother to call his father "Dad." Over the last several months, their bond had soured due to Davian's increasingly frequent trips into the mountain caves. His father was upset by his son's constant absence and strange obsession. His mother, Lia, was also not pleased that Davian had quit his job and was only shirking more and more responsibilities at home and becoming a recluse. Davian didn't care; he kept on doing as he pleased, fixating on the nearby caves and thinking of nothing else.

"What?" Deacon asked as Davian approached him. Deacon focused on the scrap in his son's hand, fearful of what he might have seen, instantly regretting that he hadn't been more careful when cleaning out his study.

"What is this?" Davian repeated sternly. "This tells me that you not have been truthful with me all of these years."

"My boy, what are you talking about?" retorted Deacon.

Davian shoved the parchment in his father's face so close that it almost touched his skin. Deacon took the bit of paper from his hand and examined the words. Davian carefully watched his father's facial expression it changed from worried curiosity to defeated disappointment.

"I cannot hide this from you any longer," he stated regretfully.

"What have you been keeping from me?" accused Davian. "The knowledge of dragons? This is the power that I have been seeking for years!"

"I am sorry, son," replied Deacon.

Anger began to creep into Davian's heart. He was furious with his father. "Don't call me that! You know how hard I have slaved over books, slaved in those caves, to learn more about this!" he cried. "What else have you been keeping from me!?"

"Please do not be angry with me," said Deacon, feeling guilty as the look of hurt and frustration grew across his son's pale face. "I did not tell you yet because I was afraid that if you learned of this too early, you would not be able to avoid the dark side of its power. I worry because I love you-"

"Don't try to justify your actions with excuses now!" Davian shouted. "You've lied to me my entire life! How am I supposed to think that you're not fabricating everything you're saying at this moment!?"

"Please believe me, son. Many others as bright and ambitious as you have lost their way, intoxicated with its power," Deacon stated sorrowfully. "As you already know, cigam can become very addictive. The dragons have much more power even than us humans. Trust me; I know you, my son. I love you and I'm proud of you. But you are never satisfied with your level of knowledge and intelligence—so much so that I feared I would lose you to your hunger."

"You may lose me now for sure!" responded Davian angrily. "You should have *believed* in me! I am your son, and you *betrayed* me!"

Deacon gritted his teeth against his son's shouting. "I

never meant to hurt you, Davian. You know that I love you-"

"You don't love me and you were never proud of me. You weren't trying to protect me at all; you were just jealous and afraid of me! You always have been!" Davian cried, finally admitting his lifelong suspicions.

"That is not true!" Deacon argued. "Listen to reason, Davian!"

"I've *always* been better than you. Better than you and everyone else on this forsaken island," growled Davian. "If you want to make it up even the slightest bit to me after all these years of betrayal, you will tell me where I can learn about the dragons and how to use their power," offered the angry young man.

"Please, son. I don't want to lose you," Deacon begged.

"You have already lost me, old man!" he roared. "Now tell me before I really lose my temper! Infirm or not, I may strike you down where you stand, for how furious I am right now!"

Deacon shook his head sadly. "There is an old cigamian on the outskirts of town, in the lodge by the tall pines. If you tell him that I sent you, he will accept you as his pupil and teach you everything."

"Perfect. I will go immediately."

"Son," Deacon pled again, "please, do not leave us! Your old mother and father..." He hung his head sadly. "But if you feel you must, please just do not let the power control you. Do not lose sight of who you are now."

Davian scoffed. "Who I am now? Forget who I am *now*. I plan on becoming the most power cigamian in the world! No thanks to you." He glared icily at his father with narrowed eyes. "And I am sick and tired of you fretting about the power controlling me. *Nothing* controls me. Remember that."

He turned promptly, leaving his father in the garden and headed inside the house, hurrying up to his room on third floor.

Deacon watched his son leave, knowing that the worst could happen. "My son is gone," he mourned.

Davian returned downstairs after gathering his

belongings for his journey. His father was waiting tearfully for him in the entry, looking pallid and breathless. Feeling a twinge of guilt, he turned to Deacon and said, "Father, I'll come back when I am done. I'll take care of you and Mother when I am able. I must go now."

And with that, he set off.

Davian left the front porch and began down the path towards the main road. "This man will also probably have knowledge about dragons—where they are and how to handle them," he murmured to himself.

He imagined himself taming one, or two, or a dozen of the scaly beasts for his control and felt excited, quickening his pace. He then felt frustrated as he continued to think, "Actually, this cigamian may be an old coward like my father and not teach me everything I want. I will have to make sure that he tells me everything he knows. And if he refuses, I'll kill him!" Then he thought, "Once he teaches me everything he knows, I may just have to kill him anyway, to be safe."

In the meantime, Davian reached the main road and headed south. Several other townsfolk walked in both directions on the main road, minding their own business and not paying the young man much heed. A few halflings passing by gave a curt nod in recognition. Davian nodded back and continued toward the cigamian's lodge.

While he continued on this path, his mother reached the steps leading up to the house, no more than ten minutes after Davian had left. Sensing something amiss, she reached the front door, opened it and entered.

Lia returned to find her husband Deacon sitting in his favorite cushioned armchair in the living room. The way he was laying back on the chair was all wrong. He sat slumped and deathly still, head bowed onto his chest and arms limp. He appeared to be dead.

Lia stopped short and dropped her bags of groceries to rush over to kneel at his side.

"Deacon!" she screamed.

He let loose a deep sigh and stirred. Realizing he was

yet alive, she gently took his head in her arms and asked him what had happened.

"He... he is... *gone!*" Deacon stammered. "He's gone! Our only son is gone!" exclaimed the old man as he began to sob anew.

"You scared me out of my wits!" Lia said to him, her heart still pounding. "As I came into the room, I thought that you were dead!"

"I might as well be dead now," he said sorrowfully. "If I were dead, none of this would have happened."

"What are you talking about?" Lia asked softly. She continued to hold him and stroke his face as she wiped the tears away.

"I told him..." Deacon gasped. "I told him about the dragons! He found a piece of one of my old manuscripts and made me tell him. He even threatened to kill me, he was so angry!"

Lia gasped in shocked. "I can't believe it... You know what could happen," she tells him.

"I know, I know," Deacon replied in anguish. "It is all my fault. Had he not found the paper, it would have been fine. I was careless."

"Hush, dear. It is all right. Just calm yourself," Lia crooned reassuringly.

Deacon was quiet for a moment. "It is time for us to leave."

Lia looked at him, puzzled. "What do you mean, dear?"

Her husband's eyes were full of fear. "If we are still here when he returns, I fear he may kill us."

"What are you saying? Whatever for?" she asked incredulously.

"You didn't see how angry he was, Lia. He was furious that we kept the information from him."

"Even so, you don't think Davian would have any compassion for his own parents?"

"I fear the worst," said Deacon. "Especially after he returns with the power he gains."

"All right, I'll start packing tonight," she stated sadly. "How long do you think we have before he returns?"

"With how quick he can learn? Six months at the most."

Her shoulders slumped as she glanced around their home and sighed. "Well, we cannot do anything on an empty stomach," Lia concluded. "I'll go and prepare dinner first."

CHAPTER SIX: HOMECOMING

Six months later, Davian did return home. He instinctively headed towards the garden in the back of the large multi-winged house. It had evidently been left unattended. The yards in front of and behind the house, usually filled with freshly-cut lawns, blooming flowers, and manicured topiaries were now overrun with weeds and vines, and the plants were all overgrown. The vegetable garden out back was a dried up mess, the ground speckled with rotting fruits and vegetables that had never been picked. Worms and other insects had made their home in them. The entire place looked abandoned.

The young man had been so confident with himself on his walk home. Davian felt smug thinking over all the things he had learned that no one else knew about. He'd been so fixated on coming back and showing off his newfound knowledge and abilities, that he never thought for a moment that anything might have gone wrong back at home. His father should have been working in the garden and his mother should have been preparing dinner on the stove at this time of day. Clearly, this was not the case.

In the sky, the sun began to descend, casting long shadows behind everything. Fearing the worst, Davian broke into a run towards the front door. His mind ran through several scenarios of what might have happened to his parents.

"If anyone has hurt them, they will pay dearly!" he swore aloud.

The door groaned in response as it swung open. The place was dark, cold, and empty. No fire warmed the wintry cold house, so his breath fogged before him. Hearing nothing and growing more anxious, Davian entered the living room. In front of him were several trunks and bags of various sizes. They were scattered around, all in disarray.

"What's this?"

The baggage was strewn throughout the great room

between the once lavish furniture which was now covered in spider webs and dust. Davian's eyebrows arched sharply. Had they been robbed?

"Mother? Father!?" he yelled. "Are you all right? Is anyone home?" Davian pounded through to the dining room and kitchen, finding only lonely pots and pans. "Is anyone here...?"

Davian felt a vague twisting in his chest as silence continued to greet him. Feeling as empty as the house he stood in, the young man approached one of the trunks and slid the lid off, allowing it to fall to the floor. It hit the wooden floor with a resounding thud that echoed throughout the lonely room, straight into his heart.

"Clothes?"

Seeing that the chest was full of his mother's clothes, he then he walked over to another large box and budged it with his foot. It was heavy. He shoved the top off and looked inside. This time, he found his parents' silverware and fine dining set. Gilded with real gold and silver, some utensils with handles encrusted with gems, the silverware was worth a pretty penny. No robber would have left it behind like this.

"...Did they leave?" he asked himself. Davian immediately looked up from the box and, with greater urgency, headed upstairs.

CHAPTER SEVEN: THE GODS

Gradually, The Creator began to worry about some of the peoples' usage of cigam. A few were using their abilities to trick, hurt or steal from others. The Creator watched these crimes with sadness and disappointment, but would not budge from his divine vow. He could not lift a finger to stop the crooks and villains from abusing his gift. The people below would have to solve the problems in their world themselves.

However, it wasn't long before the Shadower named Davian developed an uncanny ability to absorb other peoples' cigam and influence masses of people, accumulating innumerable followers. Davian's twisted kingdom would grow—some subjects willing and many others only following out of fear. Each day, fewer and fewer were able to challenge him.

The world he created was threatening to unravel at the seams. The Creator couldn't let that happen. It was more than just any simple world; he loved the land and the people. It was the place he called home and no one man could be allowed to rule and destroy it all.

The Creator agonized over how to intervene in his world without breaking his old vow, but there was no way to stop Davian without breaking his promise...

From an unfathomable distance, the Creator watched the scene with dismay. It was unavoidable. He knew that the one who had the best chance of changing the direction of this destructive path lived in another world. The boy's innocence and commitment were but a few of the traits needed to thwart this impending evil. His sincerity and goodness would allow the cigam to flow through his heart and convince even the greatest of dragons to obey him. This special person was Lorenzo, otherwise known as Lorenz in this land.

Lorenzo's, or Lorenz's, mind had to return to his home world ever so often in order to allow his soul to recharge, as the time spent traveling in this realm was very taxing on another's spiritual energy. In fact, the only way to travel between the two worlds was to use the gem in his pocket, which was why the Creator had sent it to him, as his master, Lerasus, instructed.

The god, Lerasus, brightest and most adventurous of all, was the most open-minded of the gods, and it was he who created the gem. It was also Lerasus who had made the Creator, who in turn had made and watched over Lorenz's two worlds. Noticing the gradual imbalance in the flow of cigam, Lerasus had decided that he wanted a method for the beings of one world to be able to travel to another, which was why he planned to forge the gem.

The other gods, ever self-serving, did not agree. They feared the notion of giving the lesser beings the powers of the gods. They threatened to ostracize Lerasus from the pantheon if he made such a thing. Lerasus, determined to carry out his plan, remained quiet about his intentions, yet hoped that the other gods would gradually turn in favor if his idea. Meanwhile, his plan was to hide the gem from everyone. He gave the gem to the Creator, his protégé, for safekeeping. He knew that the gods would not see it with him.

Siding with Lerasus, the Creator was happy to conceal the gem in his domain until he found a suitable owner. He had billions of beings to choose from—billions of souls to search until his found the right mixture of ardor, humility and innocence. And when the Creator decided that Lorenz would be the one to challenge the malevolence of Davian, he sent the gem down to him.

And Lorenz did not disappoint. He did exactly as the Creator had hoped.

Now, the real challenge was to ensure that this special one would succeed.

CHAPTER EIGHT: THE MEN OF FATE

Upon leaving the small island in the Grey Sea in favor of the country's mainland, the young man, Davian's, infamy grew rapidly and soon many people feared even the mention of his name. Throughout the years, he created havoc in all the land of Gene, his home country, and once done with that, he made every effort to expand his influence to other cities and nations as well. Absorbing countless victims' energies, he left weeping widows and smoldering ruins in his wake and kidnapped cigam-wielding children to brainwash them into joining his villainous crew.

One family in particular was very wary of Davian's growing power and influence. The Vrystallic family in the nearby land of Bexo was well known and respected. They'd been hailed as excellent cigamians for over a century and now they faced the ultimate test. As Davian's power grew, so did the Vrystallics' intent on stopping him.

Rusty (short for Rustico) was a youthful and hot-blooded member of the Vrystallic family. He knew Davian's intent—to take over his homeland and steal the life and liberty from his people. To prevent this, he gathered as many cigamians as well as other skilled technicians and warriors to join him in his stand against Davian. Aware of this, Davian focused on bolstering his own dark clan of subdued followers. A major standoff would soon occur.

Rusty knew that it was important to stop Davian now, before he became too great, or the world as they knew it could be lost. Knowing that many would die facing Davian and his cohorts, he prepared his family for the ordeal.

Recently a new little shining star had been born into Rusty's household—a baby boy named Thiek. It was clear that the child was special. He had a gift, the innate talent to use cigam. Even at the tender age of four, Thiek was learning faster than anyone else his age, or even years beyond his age. It became clear protecting him was important, especially with the knowledge that a large-scale battle was inevitable and the Vrystallics might not succeed.

"I have to send Thiek to a place no one knows, where no one will find him," Rusty said to himself.

Rusty built a house in the middle of a wild mountainous forest, far from the reaches of any evil-doers. Wanting the boy's location to be an absolute secret, he did not even tell the other members of his family where the house was.

He entrusted an old wise man to watch the home and child in his absence. This old man was Yoshi, a longtime friend who was very knowledgeable in cigam. Though he was seasoned in his years and his abilities had therefore waned, Rusty knew that Yoshi would not let him down.

One fateful night when he was ready, Rusty woke his wife Rose from slumber and explained what he needed to do with their son. She immediately understood and acquiesced, yet not without great sadness and concern. She, also a skilled cigamian herself, kissed the infant Thiek on the forehead ever so tenderly. She gave both Rusty and her child a tearful hug goodbye and watched as her husband left, carrying their son away. With Davian's war on the horizon, she knew that she might never see either of them again.

Rusty slipped out of the house and headed for the safety of the home he built in the wilderness. The journey was quick. Knowing no place was entirely safe because of Davian's forces, he travelled in the shadows and the brush, making sure to avoid the notice of anyone. Using all of the shortcuts he knew, the journey still took several days. The two arrived safely at the house where they were greeted by the elderly guardian.

Rusty quickly dropped Thiek into his arms without many words. Yoshi knew what he had to do.

"Go now," ordered the old man.

Rusty quickly obeyed, leaving the safe house without being noticed and he headed back home, fearing the worst.

Upon arriving home a few days later, he could sense the destruction before he could see it. No one traveled along the roads leading to town and the lingering smell of smoke hung in the air. His heart sunk with every step closer that he took. The local buildings were demolished; many of them had been burned down. Storefronts had been bashed into rubble as if by stampeding beasts; homes had been reduced to scattered bits of singed brick and wood. The once beautiful and vibrant city was now charred black by the fires that had ravaged them. Rusty fought back his terror at what he might find as he approached the remnants of what was once his and his wife's home.

"Rose... Am I too late?"

CHAPTER NINE: THE MURDERER MUST BE CAUGHT

Midday in the town of Nidum, the residents were abuzz with concern about several murders that had recently taken place. Although the townsfolk were quietly relieved that the thug Jbug and his gang of bandits were dead, they were afraid of the way that the men were murdered. The killings sounded gruesome. The bodies were sliced open viciously; severed hands and blood was splattered all over. What was most disturbing was that all three of the men were killed in the same house during the same time. Whoever had done it must have been a real brute.

People in town speculated that it could have been the work of a rival gang. No one had ever observed a scene like this before. Curious folk would pass by staring or crowd around to gawk as the police investigated the scene and carried out the bodies. The corpses were covered with white sheets, but everyone around could smell the death in the air as they were wheeled away. By the time local law enforcement knew to investigate the crime, the three men had clearly been long dead from their injuries.

The hideout had been cleared out earlier that morning after a door-to-door traveling salesman had come up to the house to peddle his wares. Upon approaching the front door, which was eerily ajar, he could clearly smell the stench of rotting meat, and had hurriedly left the scene to ask authorities to investigate.

As the town sheriff, Dingle had been assigned to check on the murder scene. He knew the house and the people who lived in it and prepared for the worst. He was a methodical investigator and took every step slowly and carefully, taking down notes as he observed things. As he'd been told, the front door of the building was indeed slightly ajar. In all the times he had been called to this place to investigate disappearances and robberies, the doors to the house had never been left unlocked. Everything else seemed normal upon first glance. The furniture and other things were in their usual place as far as he could remember.

He was about to call out, but before he could mouth any words, a foul odor reached his nostrils. His hand went cautiously to the sword at his side. He slowly approached the stairwell and looked up into the darkness. Then, careful not to make another sound, he climbed the stairs.

With each step, he assessed his surroundings. Approaching to top floor, just over to the banister at his right, he saw a sight that made him gasp. It appeared to be someone's body. It was turned away from him so that he couldn't recognize who it was. He inched forward and took a closer look at the prone object.

Making sure not to touch the foul-smelling body, he realized it was Jbug's associate, Nathanu. It is pretty clear that he had been dead for a few days. Blowflies darted across his livid skin and maggots crawled about the leaking eye sockets and open mouth. Dingle held back a gag and covered his mouth and nose with his sleeve, masking some of the reek.

He spotted another body just feet away in the open bedroom next to Nathanu. He walked closer and peeked into the room.

"What a mess!" he exclaimed. "A mass murder? I need to find out who did this! They didn't deserve to die like this, slaughtered and left like garbage for the worms to eat."

The bodies of Mannu and Jbug were strewn across the floor in what had previously been pools of their blood—now a dry, brown, crusty mess. There were pieces of a broken table across the ground and the bed covers were all in disarray. A real struggle had taken place.

Dingle saw that Mannu's cause of death was most likely the wide, deep gash in his right thigh. It exposed the bone and sinew, and clearly had opened up his veins and arteries, causing him to bleed out. The severity of the wound was clear even despite the bloating of the fetid flesh and the larvae crawling through it.

"It must have been an especially sharp sword to have cut him so deep and cleanly," Dingle surmised.

He turned away from Mannu to have a closer look at Jbug. He was lying on side, curled up in the fetal position. The right hand had been completely severed and was lying on the floor a few feet away. Dingle looked away in disgust.

"I wonder if the killer left any trace?" he wondered. "I just can't let this be."

He started looking for clues, checking the bodies again and then turning to carefully search the rest of the house. Upon leaving the grotesque scene in the bedroom, he noticed a footprint of dried blood on the floor near Nathanu's corpse.

He closely examined the print as best he could. "Judging from the size, it was left by a man's boot," he concluded. "I wonder if it could have been that young man I saw walking with Jbug the other day. He might know something."

Dingle continued to search the house, but found no other helpful clues. The rest of the house seemed to be in order. Nothing else seemed damaged or stolen, which meant that they hadn't been killed by robbers.

He had to find that young stranger and get to the bottom of this.

CHAPTER TEN: LORENZ'S LESSON

Thiek smiled as Lorenz successfully finished mixing the ingredients for the healing spell he was practicing. The bwasan leave poultice looked perfect, just like in the diagrams in the book. The old mentor walked over to the kitchen counter and picked up a knife as the young man watched, wondering what on earth he was doing.

"Thiek, what's the big knife for?" Lorenz asked.

Thiek shrugged. "It's time to see if you were successful."

Now aware of what the old man was planning, Lorenz felt his heart stiffen with fear. "Wait! What are you doing!? What if it doesn't work?"

"I'll be alright," reassured Thiek.

With his right hand, Thiek quickly dragged the blade across his left forearm, causing blood to start trickling from the wound. He didn't so much as blink all the while. The old man sure was tough. He then wiped the blade clean and placed it back on the counter. The rivulets of blood thickened and flowed as Thiek brought himself closer to Lorenz, his protégé. Not feeling nearly as confident as Thiek seemed to be, he prayed silently to myself that the spell would work.

"Alright Lorenz, recite your spell," said Thiek. "Don't leave me bleeding here. I'll make a mess of the kitchen floor."

His words made the student cringe. Lorenz gingerly rubbed the herbal poultice onto the open wound without so much as a wince from the old man. He picked up his wand and chanted the spell in his head a few times first to practice and then readied himself to recite for real.

Pointing the long wooden wand at Thiek's wound, he held the stick just inches away from his flesh, and said the incantation. At first, nothing seemed to happen and the blood continued to flow, but then he noticed that the bleeding began to slow until it nearly stopped altogether.

"Wow, this is really working!" he thought to himself. Though he kept his surprise silent, his mouth fell open to betray his true feelings.

"Keep focused," commanded Thiek, noticing the distracted look on the boy's face. "You don't want to leave me with an ugly scar, do you?" he joked.

Refocusing his attention, Lorenz finally erased the wound from Thiek's skin. The edges of the wound met and sealed themselves together, and the scar tissue faded and disappeared. It was as if it had never been there to begin with.

"It's like you never cut yourself at all!" he rejoiced.

"Good work, lad! I knew you could do it," Thiek exclaimed happily. "I'm very proud of you. You kept focused and completed the spell perfectly. How do you feel?"

"I feel fine. I'm really happy that I completed my first spell," the exhilarated student answered. He didn't know what to think or feel. He actually hadn't really believed that he could do it and that he'd end up having to help Thiek bandage up his arm.

"When reciting spells, your own energy is expended. How much is spent depends on the spell's level of difficulty," Thiek explained. "When most people perform their first spell, they usually feel a bit fatigued. This is natural."

"Wow," exclaimed Lorenz. But the boy was too excited to feel tired. "I just wish my mom could see me now," he exclaimed.

"Why don't you go upstairs and get your notes. We can try some of the next couple of spells," suggested Thiek.

"Okay, I guess we'll need more ingredients," Lorenz replied, gesturing at the pieces of plants that they'd already ground up for the healing enchantment.

"Don't worry. I grow the herbs we need in the backyard," said Thiek.

"Alright."

Lorenz nodded and headed to his room to get his things as his teacher watched him proudly as he left.

"Davian, you will meet your match!" the old man exulted quietly.

Seeing Lorenz hurry away so eagerly after his first

spell caused Thiek to reminisce on the old days when he himself was a strapping young lad, still learning about the world. How similar the boy seemed to learn from his teacher! His offhand comment about his mother had awoken something—a sad but sweetly nostalgic reminder. Thiek remembered terribly missing his own parents as he studied cigam with his mentor.

Thiek silently went about the kitchen, cleaning up the bowls and utensils they'd used to prepare the bwasan leaves for the healing poultice. Then he began gathering the tools and ingredients for the next spells he intended to go over. As he did so, a bit of anger bubbled up from his core as he remembered learning how Davian had destroyed his family. He had been forced to live in hiding for years after his family had been murdered in order to avoid Davian's men who'd been trying to find and kill him.

"Now, Davian's time is limited thanks to Lorenz!" he thought to himself.

He'd have to teach him all the spells in the books and make sure that he understood how to use them to their full potential. That was their only hope—if Lorenz could maximize the spell's powers. Thiek knew that the cigamian who had trained Davian did not teach him the deepest levels of spell usage, how to become one with the spells' essences, for that would have made Davian even more powerful.

"I just have to be careful not to push Lorenz too fast."

Thiek vividly remembered watching when his father desperately battled Davian for his life. They whirled in their robes, bursts of hot light flying from their pointed wands. His father had finally gotten a good blow in and knocked the wand from Davian's hand. So close to victory, seeing the angry look of defeat in Davian's eyes, his father was suddenly ambushed from behind. And hidden away in the thick brush about thirty feet away, young Thiek saw his father die.

Unable to fight off the four men by himself, struck again and again, with blood pouring from his mouth and nose, he fell to his knees. Thiek watched Davian retrieve his dropped wand, raise his hands and say something that he could not understand. He remembered watching as his father's body froze, as if paralyzed in invisible ice.

Thiek's heart raced as he prayed for someone to help them and he saw Davian get a sword from the henchman standing next to him. He raised it high into the air with a haughty sneer, and brought it down on Thiek's father's neck, severing his bowed head all in one vicious swoop. His father's head tumbled to the ground. It took everything within the boy, Thiek, to keep silent. Pain filled his entire body almost to the point losing consciousness. His mind grew fuzzy; he felt dizzy and sick as he remained crouched in the bushes, with his tears falling silently from his face. He could feel his heart breaking and his body being overwhelmed by not only pain, but a deep engulfing hatred that he could never before have expected.

"I will never rest until my father's murder is avenged," Thiek proclaimed to himself. "The world must be rid of this evil."

CHAPTER ELEVEN: TWO BROTHERS AND A TAVERN

In the land of Geuter, the lower region of Waealand, the adventure continues.

Unni and Okin, two dwarves, entered the town of Wortheast. Lorenz was hard at work studying at Thiek's home as the dwarves headed for a local tavern. The city was much larger than they expected. The dwarven brothers surveyed the hustle and bustle around them as they traveled. Dozens of people shuffled by them on either side. People were out shopping, working, or eating at the vast array of small and large buildings. The delicious smells of grilled meat met their nostrils as they passed by a restaurant with an open-air seating area where many couples and families dined. Carts and carriages pulled by various draft animals rumbled and clopped by on the streets.

"Big horses here, brother," pointed out Unni in dwarvish tongue. Though they were fluent in English and a few other languages thanks to their years of travel, the two usually spoke in their native dwarvish language to one another.

"Yeah, it'd be hard for us to ride them," agreed Okin with a laugh. The huge animals stood at least five or six feet tall. Each standing at less than four feet themselves, it would be a pain for them to mount and dismount from such tall horses. "We'd have to find smaller draft animals to ride during our journey."

"We'll ask around," replied Unni.

"Let's go in here. I'm sure we can find some information," Okin suggested as they approached a nearby tavern.

On the front of the building, hanging from the roof, was a wooden triangular sign that read "Wirgin." They climbed the small steps leading onto the porch-like entry of the tavern and entered the doors. Inside, they found several patrons drinking, laughing, and just milling about.

A stout human man with a round face and protruding

belly walked right past Unni. Okin noticed that he gave Unni a strange sidelong look. He stopped short, wondering about the man's expression until his brother called him over.

They approached the bar which stood approximately three and a half feet high, just a couple of inches above Unni's head. Behind the bar, two people serviced the customers. One bartender was a woman in her thirties with long brown hair. She was broad-framed and dressed modestly in a plain tunic and apron. The other bartender was a skinny man of average height, around forty years old. He was dressed in a brown blouse and belted black slacks that were a few sizes too big for his scrawny legs and waist.

Scattered throughout the tavern were various dining tables and bar stools. The dwarves looked around the bar for a good place to sit. Before they had the chance to make up their minds, a server whizzed past them carrying a tray of bronze goblets and called out to them, "Welcome to Wirgin! Sit anywhere ya want!"

"There's a table over there," proposed Okin to his brother in dwarvish.

They sat themselves at the empty table near the far side of the bar after putting their bags and weapons on the ground under their table. Being in a human city, the chairs were much taller than they would have preferred and their legs dangled from the seats uncomfortably. Within minutes, the same server came by to assist them.

"Can-ah we jus' order summa dark ale?" asked Okin in his thick accent.

"Comin' right up!" the waiter replied and walked away. It didn't take long for him to fill up some glasses at the bar and bring it back to the brothers. "Dark ale for two!"

Okin and Unni thanked him and took welcome swigs of their drinks, as they had gotten thirsty after all their walking around town. They would rest up here before gathering more supplies for their journey and meeting up with their friend, Lorenz, once again.

CHAPTER TWELVE: LORENZ'S FEAR

Upstairs, Lorenz reached the door to his room and opened it. He was smiling and there was a spring in his step, as he recalled his first real spell. He almost felt as if he were glowing, for how happy and excited he felt.

He walked inside the room, reaching for a spell book on the bookshelf by the left wall. Without warning, swirling darkness began to overtake his sight.

"It's happening again," he thought to himself.

Having experienced this many times before, he no longer felt alarmed or uncomfortable by the transition. The nauseating twisting in his stomach was more of a flutter now and even his sight seemed clearer than it previously had been while moving between worlds.

In a few short moments, he was on his feet and took in his new surroundings. After a few moments, he recognized where he was and what had happened. He was fifteen years old and he now stood in front of his new school.

His mother had chosen a new school that was further away, but very highly acclaimed for its extracurricular programs and awards. The campus was also very clean and safe. This caused him to think about the school that he was otherwise supposed to attend, around the corner from his house, and the other places he'd been to before.

"I would have been constantly bullied there the whole time. There were always fights at that school. I'm so happy that I got to go here."

It was hard to get into this high school because so many people in the area applied to it. He and his mom were thrilled when they received the acceptance letter.

Lorenzo had been standing at the entrance of the school for only a few seconds as he reminisced before he realized that it was time to go in. He took one last look at his surroundings before heading towards the double doors.

The school building looked kind of like a refurbished firehouse. A huge, red bricked, rectangular monolith, it was the only building of its kind on the block. The neighborhood around it could be described as similar to a small college town. There was a café, bookstore, and a park near the school campus that students, teachers, and others would frequent.

The atmosphere was pleasant and laid back. Fellow schoolmates ate lunch on the benches under the trees in the courtyard. Others browsed the bookstore for textbooks and school supplies. Just looking around his surroundings caused Lorenzo to become excited.

It was now about 8:30 in the morning. Birds chirped from the trees in the park and the morning was cool and refreshingly breezy. A couple of people had passed him and he finally began to head up the cement stairs towards the big black double doors. There were a couple of students and staff entering ahead of him. The last, a blond curly-haired boy held the door open for Lorenzo with a polite smile.

Lorenzo thanked him and as soon as he entered the building, he immediately stopped. He heard the doors creaking as they closed. The enormously tall ceilings stretched out before him as he looked up. As he slowly walked forward, he surveyed the walls. They were unusually yellow and papered with various posters, paintings, as well as other framed school awards. And to his left appeared to be a classroom; to his right was an office.

Directly in the front of him were more classrooms. Class was starting soon, so he started searching for his room. Other students were walking around him to their various destinations as he stood looking stupefied.

Lorenzo walked forward a bit until he spotted another set of double-doors leading to some stairs that went either direction. As he approached, he noticed the numbers above the doors of the different classrooms. He pulled out his class schedule from his pocket. He hadn't memorized his class line up yet since it was only his first day here. It indicated that his first class was Biology in room 101. There it was. He shifted his backpack on his shoulders and headed towards the room.

He walked through the room entrance. Inside, the

room was arranged very differently. Instead of individual pressboard desks, there were long black countertops. The plastic and metal chairs were lined up along the counters and many of the students were already seated in them. In the center of the room was a tall console with various glass items, one of which was a lushly planted fish tank. It was surrounded by numerous glass jars filled with preserved specimens of curious-looking creatures.

Lorenzo quickly looked around for a chair that was situated away from the others. He found one close to one of the walls.

"Perfect."

He headed for the empty seat, passing some other students along the way. "No one grabbed my hair this time like that one girl did in junior high," he mused. Now comfortable, he placed his backpack on the floor.

Lorenzo looked around, and then pulled out a notebook and pencil.

A thin man who seemed to be almost six and a half feet tall entered the room right as the school bell rang, indicating the commencement of classes for the day. He walked to the front of the class and faced the students. Behind him was a large chalkboard with "Biology" written in the top left-hand corner.

"Good morning, class," said the tall lanky teacher jovially as he put on a pair of spectacles.

A few students mumbled good morning back, but mostly the class was buzzing with students' conversations. People were also texting on their cellphones or getting their papers and pens out.

Just as Lorenzo opened up his notebook, he felt his pocket vibrate. Immediately, he knew what was about to happen. It was time to travel back again. He groaned quietly to himself in disappointment, as he was looking forward to seeing what the class would be like.

As his sight began to fade, he wondered how much time would pass before he was able to come back. He took a deep breath. The spinning he experienced that once made him dizzy was now like a rollercoaster ride he had learned to enjoy. Before he knew it, the spinning began to die down and his eyes began to clear.

He landed. He was standing right outside of his room at Thiek's house and, surprisingly enough, still had his wand and spell book in hand. He vaguely remembered something about retrieving the spell book for Thiek and continued downstairs.

"I can't wait to practice these new spells!" he told himself.

Once downstairs, he found Thiek waiting for him in the kitchen.

"Did you get everything?"

"Yes I did," Lorenz replied.

"Good." Thiek nodded. "Now, I want you to go out into the backyard. There, you will find the ingredients for the spells we are going to work on next. What spells are listed at this level?" he asked.

"'Remove Fear,' 'Squelch Flames,' and 'Dispel Curses,'" replied Lorenz.

"Alright. The ingredients for all those spells are there. I know that you will be able to find them on your own, so I will not tell you where they are," Thiek said to him.

"That's funny," Lorenz said and chuckled to himself when he thought about it. "I kind of knew where they were anyway. In the past, I would've asked myself how I knew these things, but now I no longer feel the need to ask."

Lorenz was about to go outside to collect the herbs when Thiek smiled at him distantly and patted the chair beside him.

"Lorenz, come and have a seat before you go out and find the ingredients."

At Thiek's request, he took hold of a wooden chair and pulled it out from under the table. He looked into Thiek's eyes, wondering what he was calling him over for.

"Lorenz, it is time for me to tell you about someone you

will one day meet. Do you remember when I mentioned the name 'Davian' to you?" he continued.

"Yes."

"He is a very dangerous person. He is very powerful and he has been around for a long time—even before me."

Lorenz looked surprised. Thiek was such a little old man. It was hard to believe that there was another cigamian out there who was even older and more powerful than him. He wondered what Davian could possibly look like.

"You wouldn't know it by his looks," Thiek added. "He has learned—through cigam—how to maintain a relatively youthful body."

Lorenz assumed he meant more youthful than how Thiek looked. The grey hair and wrinkles were not kind to his appearance.

Thiek let out a slow breath and continued. "Many years ago, when he was but a young lad, he was not too different from you. He was quite an intelligent and lonely child who felt that he didn't fit in with the people around him.

"Not many people had yet become skilled in the ways of cigam. Initially, he was not a top tier cigamian like he is now. Yet, somehow he found an incredibly skilled teacher and learned to use cigam, and use it well. Being so smart, he learned very fast, like you.

"The story goes that after he returned from learning cigam from this wise man, he killed his teacher and parents. Their bodies were never found. What most people feared was that he would use his power for evil, rather than good. The story states that his parents never wanted to teach him about advanced cigam or dragons for that very reason."

Lorenz, still listening, asked, "Why will I meet him?"

"You will meet him because he will seek you out as he seeks out all of those who are strong in the ways of cigam," replied Thiek. "You must be very careful."

Lorenz cringed mentally. He didn't want to face someone like that.

"No need to be afraid," reassured Thiek, as if he had read

Lorenz's thoughts. "When you face him, you will be ready. It is because of him that I lost my family."

"What happened?" questioned Lorenz, suddenly wondering if it was appropriate for him to ask, but Thiek did not mind.

"When I was born, my father took me far away in order to protect me. He took me away from the battle initiated by Davian and his band of followers. His plan was to take over the region, and one day, even the world. My parents and relatives, who were very wealthy and influential people at the time, were not going to sit back and let this happen.

"Negotiating with Davian was out of the question. All the representatives who had to misfortune of being sent to speak with him either wound up dead or in his service. And so, the war began.

"Besides my family, there were several other cigamian families who joined forces to stop him, but they were crushed," said Thiek.

Lorenz looked on in amazement. "How could one man get so powerful?" he thought.

"He wanted all power," Thiek answered his thoughts. "He wanted to be lord over all the land, over everyone. He wanted everyone to follow him. My father was one of the few warriors who survived. It was he and his best friend who were able to teach me everything I know now."

Listening to Thiek talk about his family made Lorenz feel awful. It reminded him of when he was younger and his mother was not around and how he missed her. It reminded him of his cold aunt and his father who had abandoned him and the abusive brute whom his mother dated shortly.

Lorenz felt angry for Thiek's family and wanted to make Davian pay for his actions, even though he knew that revenge was wrong and that his powers were not meant for retaliation. But he wanted to do something for Thiek's behalf because of the kindness the old mentor had shown him.

Again, Thiek sensed Lorenz's feelings and said, "Taking revenge is not a good idea; the use of cigam for evil leads down the slippery slope of corruption. We cannot change the past. We can only protect the future of our realm."

"It's not fair that evil people can cause such great harm to others and not suffer for it," complained Lorenz bitterly. "It seems as if evil always has the upper hand and suffers no consequences for it. Bad people don't care about the results of what they do! Well, evil is not going to always get away with everything. It will pay a price."

"Lorenz," cautioned Thiek in a stern tone, "you must be careful in your anger, or you will end up like Davian. The best you can do is conduct yourself properly to make the world a better place. You will never be able to vanquish evil from the world entirely. However, you can keep it from taking over."

Soon, the two had spent a few hours talking to one another and it was now lunchtime. "Why don't we have something to eat before you head outside?" suggested Thiek.

They had been talking for so long that Lorenz had actually forgotten all about collecting the herbs out back.

Thiek backed up his chair, stood up, and began rummaging through the wooden cupboard behind him. In it were several glazed clay dishes all arranged neatly. Thiek reached out and took a couple of plates and cups for them.

"There is one more important bit of information that you must know," he stated somberly to Lorenz. After placing the plates on the table, one in front of each of their seats, he continued. "You may have heard something about the dragons. I think I mentioned them to you at one point."

"I remember," said Lorenz.

"Many years ago, before man was created, there were dragons. These creatures were not only beautiful, they were immensely powerful. They possessed incredible cigamian abilities. So when mankind was created, they naturally wanted to control the few dragons that remained on the earth. Legend has it that shortly after man's creation, most dragons were destroyed."

While talking, Thiek poured a pitcher of fresh goat's milk

into the square clay cups and Lorenz's eyes were wide open as he listened to the story.

"Dragons, wow! I'd love to see one!" Lorenz said aloud.

Thiek continued to prepare lunch while talking about the dragons. On the table he placed a bowl filled with bread as well as a large platter arranged with an assortment of cured meats. Looking at the food caused Lorenz to realize how hungry he was.

"This looks good!"

Thiek gestured towards the food and without hesitation, Lorenz dug in.

CHAPTER THIRTEEN: AT THE COVE

Still in the tavern, Unni and Okin talked amongst themselves. While they complained to each other about the lack of work, their server noticed that their glasses were almost empty.

"More ale?" the waiter asked.

"Ya, anotha round," agreed Unni.

The server began to get the drinks when Okin asked him, "We're lookin' fo' adventurin' work. Anyone inna here int'rested?"

The man stared at him for a moment as if to say, "Why are you asking me?" but he considered his question and quickly responded, "This is not really the place for that."

"Ya know a betta place for it-ah, then?" Okin continued.

The man leaned over towards Okin to say to him, "If you two are looking for work, I recommend you go down to Jinger's Cove a ways down the road. You'll find buyers there." And with that, he sped off to continue bussing the busy tables.

"What was that all about?" whispered Unni in dwarvish.

"He was telling me where to go to get some work. We should go down the road to the Jinger Cove."

"Okay," said Unni. "We should go then."

They both took the last gulp of their drinks. The dwarves rose from their high seats, left a tip for their waiter and then headed for the door. As they walked away, Okin glanced back toward the far side of the tavern to see a serious-looking man eyeing them from the corner.

"Come on," urged Unni, holding the door for his brother.

Okin grunted and hurried out the tavern. As they descended the stairs, he mentioned the man staring at them as they left.

"Did he give us a dirty look or something?" asked Unni.

"No, but I don't like anybody staring at me," grumbled Okin. "Gives me a bad feeling."

At the base of the porch, the dwarves turned north and

headed down the main road. After walking about a block or two together, Okin sensed something out the corner of his eye—movement to the side behind him. He turned his head slightly and saw the same suspicious man he saw in the tavern, wrapped up in a big coat. He took another couple of steps and looked again, but this time, the man seemed to have disappeared.

"Is he following us?" Okin wondered. He decided to remain quiet for a bit longer to see if he spotted the man again before bringing it to Unni's attention once more. When he looked back this time, he noticed the guy shift right behind a group of people walking behind them.

"What do you keep looking at?" asked Unni.

The crowd of people dispersed at a busy intersection, but he could find no trace of the strange man.

"Nothing," replied Okin. "I thought I saw someone."

As they continued walking, Unni caught sight of a wooden building in the distance partially hidden by the trees.

"There is the tavern the waiter told us to see. Jinger Cove," announced Unni.

"Well, I hope they have food there. I'm hungry," declared Okin.

Unni grunted in acknowledgement. "Me too."

They continued down the path until they finally reached the Cove. Before heading in, Okin looked furtively back down the path to see if the man was anywhere to be seen, but all he saw were mule-drawn carts and other men, women, and children traveling about town. Maybe that guy hadn't been following them after all.

Now close to the entrance of the Cove, they saw a few people coming and going. There were not nearly as many people in this part of town as they had seen at the tavern, Wirgin. The Cove was known as a place in town where the shady people would congregate—you know, the kind that looked for trouble.

As visitors, Unni and Okin, were of course unaware of the tavern's reputation, yet they were able to sense the mood there. They approached the front door and saw that it was not a large place. It had many steps up a narrow stairway leading up to its old splintery front doors. No one could call it welcoming. The windows seemed to have a dark film on them so that seeing inside was difficult. Even the grass and weeds around the building seemed twisted and dying.

The dwarves looked around the building cautiously as they entered. Just as Okin reached for the doorknob, a tall slender man—middle-aged, dressed in dark leather armor—opened it for them as he left.

Inside the dimly lit tavern, there was a round bar in center of the room. It was circled with numerous stone stools approximately two feet from each other. Table seating and booth seating were available throughout the rest of the tavern where various characters sat and talked. The clientele was almost entirely men, and there were many humans, halflings, dwarves, and even others who appeared to have elvish features.

Behind the bar was a man fulfilling the drink and food orders. He was about six feet tall, average build, with thick, bushy eyebrows. He had a full house, but seemed to manage it all with ease. He noticed the dwarves enter and welcomed them with a booming, yet jovial voice, "Sit anywhere you like, boys!"

So they looked around and located an empty booth. Unni and Okin grabbed a space off to the right. A young, scantily-clad woman who was bussing nearby spotted them and flashed them a smile as they walked to their seats.

"Don't look at anyone too long," Unni said to his brother in dwarvish so that the woman wouldn't hear. "Don't want to give people the wrong idea."

"I know. Hopefully we'll find someone interested in hiring adventurers like us," said Okin.

Once the dwarves reached their seats, which were again too high for them, they hopped up and made themselves as comfortable as possible. The beautiful waitress gave them a minute before approaching.

"Hello!" she greeted sweetly. "My name is Keeri, and I'll be your server for this evening. Can I get you boys something to eat?"

"Ya, can-ah we get summa dark ale an' roast-ah chicken?" asked Unni.

His accent was thick, but having worked at the pub for so long, the waitress was used to hearing accents of various sorts and nodded right away. She turned to head towards the bar to place the order when Unni stopped her and said, "One more thin'. We're lookin' for adventurin' work. D'ya know anyone that-ah migh' be lookin' ta hire?"

"I'll see what I can find out," Keeri replied with a small smile and then quickly left.

A few minutes later, she was back with two cold mugs of dark ale. She placed them in front of the dwarves and assured them that their meal would be ready shortly.

"And as for your other question, see that man sitting at a table by himself? He's got on the dark coat and a pointed nose. He should be able to help you."

"Thanks," said Unni.

"You're welcome and good luck. I'd better go now and get your food," she said and made for the kitchen.

Unni and Okin looked at each other.

"Let's go see this guy," said Okin. "Finally, maybe we can get some work and make some money."

"We have to be careful though," cautioned Unni. "You never know if strangers like this can be trusted."

Okin nodded in agreement. Both dwarves left their table to talk to the mysterious man. The two were halfway over to the possible client when Okin stopped dead in his tracks.

Unni glanced at him. "What?"

"It's him! It's that guy who was following us," replied Okin distrustfully.

"What guy?"

"The guy from the other tavern who was watching us." Okin jerked his head slightly in the client's direction. "I want to know why he was following us like that."

"Not now, brother. Let's ask him about the work first," suggested Unni.

Okin did not seem thrilled with the idea and paused for a moment. "Okay," he finally replied reluctantly.

"Let me do the talking," suggested Unni. Okin nodded his head in agreement as they reached the table.

The strange man made brief eye contact with them and gestured for them to sit. They obliged by pulling out chairs and when they'd settled, the mysterious man began.

"So... I, eh, hear yer lookin' for, eh, work."

CHAPTER FOURTEEN: THE SEARCH FOR A KILLER

In his office, Dingle sat pondering where the murderer might be hiding or if he had moved on far from Nidum. He had no time to lose if he intended to catch the killer.

"I'm going out to search for a spell," he told his deputy.

"Okay, Boss," Rangle replied.

Dingle opened the door and stepped out onto the porch.

"Sheriff!" called an older scrawny man who was walking by. He was a somewhat nosy elderly man by the name of Jules, who lived just around the corner.

Dingle waved to him. "Greetings, Jules. What is it?"

"Have you seen that weird guy, Jbug, lately? I haven't seen him around for a while now. Usually him and his crazy-looking friends like to loiter around here or at Ashawa."

"Nah, you won't be seeing him around anymore," Dingle replied and shrugged. "Somebody messed him up pretty bad."

"What? Well, good riddance!" said the older man, his wrinkly face lightening with a smile. "He was a bad apple anyway."

"Well, we still need to find out who did it," stated Dingle.

"Of course, Sheriff. Any leads?" Jules asked.

"Nothing solid right now. Gonna go around town and ask some questions about the suspect. Did you see anyone unusual coming or going from Jbug's place about a week or so ago?"

"A week ago? Hmmm, lemme see..." trailed the old man. "Well, I sorta remember seeing a man I didn't know. Average build and height, nothing memorable. Not sure if he was dark-skinned or not or what his face or hair were like. It was late at night, so it was dark outside. I was just taking out my garbage, so it wouldn't stink up the house. But yes, I did see someone leaving the path from Jbug's house."

"Do you remember anything else? Any distinguishing features? What he was dressed in?" queried Dingle further.

"Not really. Again, it was dark. Sorry, Sheriff. I was just doin' my own business. Besides, I didn't think anything of it at the time."

"Well, which way was he heading? He is a suspect for murder, so it is imperative that I find and question him."

"Uh, I'm not sure," answered Jules doubtfully. "I think he went south. He wasn't a big guy though. You sayin' you think *he* did Jbug and the boys in? I can't imagine him killing anyone, much less three thugs like those boys," stated the old man.

"You can't put it past anyone, especially if they're pushed into a corner," warned Dingle, shaking his head. "Knowing Jbug, the killing was probably in self-defense. Jbug and his crew most likely attacked him first."

"I'll bet," Jules agreed. "Rotten apples, the lot of them. Criminals and scoundrels."

"But there's no proof that they did attack first or that lethal force was necessary," the sheriff retorted. "Nor is there solid evidence that Jbug or his boys actually robbed, kidnapped, or murdered anyone."

Jules rolled his eyes. "Oh yeah, I bet all those poor kids last seen with 'em just disappeared on their lonesome."

"In any case, this kind of vigilantism can't go ignored," Dingle added. "People can't just go around killing each other like that; we'd have total chaos. I need to find this man and at least get the full story behind all this."

"Just let it go!" scoffed the old man, scratching his patchy grey hair. "Why bother to even search for the guy? It's been a week, you said? He's probably long gone by now with a seven day head start! Plus, as you already said, Jbug probably deserved it. We all know the shady stuff he was doing. Why pursue this now?"

"Because, Jules, we can't let murderers on the loose."

"Well, if it was self-defense, the guy most likely doesn't kill people unless he really has to," suggested Jules.

"I just have to make sure," replied Dingle.

"Well, all right. Good luck then, Sheriff," Jules stated.

"Thanks for the help, Jules. Have a good evening."

Jules waved goodbye and returned to his daily walk in his leisurely old man's pace.

The sheriff mulled over the information that Jules had given him for a few moments. "That's right, I should check Ashawa to see if I can get any info on Jbug or the stranger there."

CHAPTER FIFTEEN: DRAGONS AND CIGAM

Back at home, Thiek was just about finished telling Lorenz another story about his family when all of sudden, the blurry vision and spinning started again. Within moments, Lorenz realized that he was traveling again. The question, of course, was where he would end up this time.

Shortly, he found himself on his feet. It took another couple of seconds before his vision began to clear up. He blinked a few times and the shadows started to become colors. Red, yellow, cream, brown and black forms began to take shape. He heard the sounds of laughter and... something else. It sounded like something hitting something else hard. There was clattering and loud rolling. His first quick thought was "Where am I?" Then, "Am I in danger?"

By the time the last doubt passed through his mind, his vision was now completely clear. He was in a bowling alley, of all places.

"Bowling...?" he wondered. He was standing amidst a couple guys, probably students in his class and in a split second, he remembered that he was still in high school and he was taking bowling for his P.E. class.

"Hurry up and get your shoes on, man," said a male voice nearby. The order came from a thin black-haired boy of average height. He told him to get a move on it since Lorenzo was holding up their game.

"Oh yeah, okay," said Lorenzo, rubbing his head a little as he looked at the counter clerk.

Lorenzo was standing before the counter where the bowling shoes were rented, but had been too stunned momentarily to order his pair.

"Size nine, please?" he asked.

Within moments, the short, older man with silver hair left and returned with the shoes. They were long and slender, rounded at the tip of the shoe. They were also boldly multi-colored: red and blue with white soles and black laces. He grabbed his shoes and headed back to lane four, where his classmates were. He stepped down into the lane to sit down on the plastic seating. After switching into his shoes, he went in search of a proper bowling ball.

Behind the plastic chairs were several shelves housing many bowling balls of various sizes, weights and colors. Lorenzo eyed several. He wanted a blue one; blue was his favorite color.

He made sure it was a good fit and weight first. He placed his fingers into the three small holes and picked up the ball, quickly testing its weight by swinging it gently with his wrist. It wasn't too heavy, so he carried it over to the lane. He placed the ball into the carousel along with the other bowling balls and shook out his arms.

Jude, the guy who had called for Lorenz to hurry up, had already entered all of their names into the computer to begin the game. While waiting for the game to start, there were conversations amongst the boys about different classes and teachers and girls.

Jude was first. He walked up to the lane, and grabbed his bowling ball, which was a red twelve-pounder. He took three brisk steps forward and hurled it down the polished wooden lane. The ball rumbled down the right side of the alley for a few feet, and then veered towards the middle in a powerful curve. Another few more seconds and finally, the ball made contact with the head pin, which spun violently and knocked into the pins behind it in a loud crash. Jude, thinking he had a strike, jumped up into the air, but upon noticing one lone pin still upright, he growled in disappointment. Simultaneously, his teammates groaned and shouted at the one stubborn pin and Jude had to settle for a spare.

A young man named Kaleb was up next, bowling at the same time as the opposing team's next player. He was a poised youth with wavy blond hair. He stepped up to the lane, grabbed his bowling ball, brought it back to his left, and tossed it forward with all of his might. It hugged the gutter until about mid-way down the alley, when it suddenly made a sharp turn to the right and made a resounding strike when it hit the pins. Excited, the boy threw his arms up in a jubilant gesture and yelled, "Yeah!, booyow!" as the pins scattered and his team celebrated with him.

Another team member, Larry, left three pins standing. He turned bitterly to Kaleb and said, "Luck. Bet you can't do it again!"

Now it was Lorenzo's turn. He stood up waiting for Kaleb to return to the seats and hi-fived him upon his return.

Lorenzo grabbed his ball at the lane and clasped it tightly in his grip. He brought it back with his right hand and flung it forward. The ball traveled through the air and it landed in the middle of the alley. Rolling ever faster, Lorenzo thinks quietly to himself, "It's going to be a strike!" And just as the anticipation reaches its peak, he felt a buzzing in his pants pocket and the familiar darkness and spinning sensation began to cloud his senses.

"No!" he grunted angrily. "Not now! I wanted my strike!"

Before long, the spinning stopped and he was sitting at the table across from a smiling Thiek. He was in mid-sentence.

"-if you can get a dragon to devote itself to you, it will make you virtually unstoppable. This is why Davian never ceases his search for a dragon. He wants it for power. Unfortunately, he is most likely strong enough to manipulate the dragon into following his command. And should he ever find one to control, even the weakest of the dragons, the world would be in grave danger."

"Why does having a dragon under one's influence make them so powerful?" asked Lorenz, getting back into the conversation and shaking the memories of the bowling alley from his mind.

"Because," responded Thiek, "a dragon not only has raw brute strength, but an incredible ability to wield cigam, as well as a long life that is spends amassing a great amount of wealth. Many search in hopes of finding a dragon and befriending it. Yet there are very few who have been able to find any, much less befriend one."

"Great, well, how can I possibly face Davian then, if he's going to control a dragon?" Lorenz asked with a shrug.

"I believe that you have the right essence within you that will allow you to find and even befriend a dragon of your own," Thiek replied.

Lorenz thought this over and remembered the dragons on the wall in his room and said aloud, "I'm not sure I want to befriend them." They seemed scary.

However, Thiek reassured his young protégé. "Once you befriend them, they are the most serene and loyal creatures you could ever encounter. You have no need to fear them. They will surely accept your sincere heart. But enough of this, we need to get back to your spells! It's gotten late as we've been chatting. You'd better collect the ingredients outside while it is still light out."

By now it was a breezy late afternoon. Lorenz looked up the names of the necessary ingredients from the book and headed to the backyard to find them. Thiek watched as Lorenz opened the door.

"See you in a few minutes," he said and smiled as his student walked out.

With the spell book under his arm, Lorenz headed outside into the sea of greenery awaiting him.

CHAPTER SIXTEEN: THE SEARCH FOR A DRAGON

In the midst of the roiling Red Sea, a ship sailed bravely from one of the small islands near Der Bay. It was a rather large ship considering the sizes of the small rural villages in the area. However, what was stranger still was that the ship was making a beeline straight for the region of sea that was avoided by everyone.

The people living on the islands of Der Bay called the area "Dragars" because the waters in this region were so treacherous that some people believed that dragons roamed the waves there. Many even claimed to have seen dragons while sailing nearby.

Sharp, jagged rocks lurked just beneath the water surface, invisible to sailors, claiming countless vessels of men foolish enough to try to shortcut through Dragars. No ship had ever been able to successfully navigate these waters. So many ships had been trapped and wrecked on these rocks that the area became infamous as a ship graveyard and a cursed, haunted place.

This particular ship was about sixty feet long and had a stark black hull with tall, wide sails of grey. It was multi-storied, with round portholes below the deck. The floors provided plenty of room for the crew to rest and store their supplies. The helm was enclosed in a rectangular windowed room from where the captain could guide the large ship. This chamber contained the ship's wheel and maps. On the deck were also numerous black barrels. There were fifteen of them, each about four feet tall. Filled with some kind of liquid, they were strategically placed throughout the deck of the ship along with several studded chests wrapped in leather bindings and iron locks.

As the sun reached its peak in the sky, the waters began to slowly stir. The captain ordered the men to lower the sails and a muscular crew of swarthy men leapt into action. They hurried to lower the sails in hopes of settling the ship. But suddenly, the waves started to froth and five to six foot swells heaved all around, rocking the ship back and forth mercilessly. Everyone stumbled in their footing as the vessel slammed up against the crags around the mysterious island they were aiming for. Standing amidst the feverishly working men was Davian.

Unconcerned with the water's threatening gestures, he surveyed the distant island before him. Dressed in a silver and black robe with tall leather boots, Davian did not fit in at all with the rest of the crew in their sailor tunics and trousers. He watched silently as the men tugged at the riggings, getting soaked in the salty spray of the angry ocean. His own clothes were wet too, but it was of no matter. They were getting close.

Much older now, Davian's once raven locks were now streaked with grey and his wrinkled face bore the permanent lines of an unhappy man. He closed his eyes to try and sense where the dragons might be.

"Over there!" he cried, pointing with his right hand. "Steer the ship in that direction."

"The waters are too dangerous, sir!" argued the captain, a tall, bearded man wearing a thick coat and wide-brimmed hat. "We risk total destruction of the ship!"

"I'll easily procure you a newer, better ship with my funds," promised Davian.

He seemed enticed and thought for a second, gauging the rocks and waves. "...We may be able to get just a little bit closer," decided the captain.

"Then do it."

They continued on course, but the waves only dashed against them against the sharp rocks even harder. Surges of water splashed onto the ship's deck, making the whole place slick and slippery. The vessel was hit so hard that it even caused some of the cargo to come loose of their bindings and slide about the ship. One barrel actually hit the side, cracking, causing a viscous blue liquid to seep out the broken barrel. The sailors worked desperately to secure the boat. Some men re-secured the loose cargo and the others continued manning the sails. The captain shouted orders while frantically trying to stabilize the ship. Davian alone stood firmly and silently despite the chaos.

"We must move the ship back, sir!" explained the captain. "She is taking on too much water and damage. We won't make it!"

"A few more minutes and we can move the ship back," reassured Davian. "I have to check for something first. Get me the telescope."

A nearby deck hand grabbed it as it rolled around the floor, which was now a flooded mess. The man handed Davian the telescope, but then slipped and fell to the deck as he walked away to help his crewmembers.

Noticing the scattered barrels, Davian commanded the men, "Hey! Secure the liquid!"

"Get that busted barrel overboard before it contaminates the ship!" yelled the captain.

Davian looked through the telescope at the island. "There it is!" he exclaimed. "We found it-!" But as soon as the words tried to leave his mouth, an incredibly massive wave struck the ship from the port side.

Davian threw his arms out and fell to his knees onto the deck, the telescope flying out of his hand and over the railing of the ship, into the dark water below. Barrels and chests slid to and fro, crashing violently into the rails of the ship as well.

Furious, Davian rose to his feet. Unnoticed by the crew, he raised his hands and quietly uttered the words: "Waves the crash, waters the rise, now calm thyself by the one who is wise."

Amazingly, within moments, and much to the surprise of those onboard, the terrible waves assaulting the ship began to cease. The captain and crew all paused and stared in awe as Davian finished speaking and lowered his arms.

"See, I told you not to worry," said Davian smugly. "Never doubt me."

"All right men, no time to dawdle! Keep securing the cargo!" ordered the captain as he snapped out of his shock.

He had no idea that cigamians could have the power to calm a raging sea; it only reaffirmed his hopes of him and the crew being handsomely rewarded by the end. But they had to stay on task. They weren't in the clear yet. The men on the ship began the ship's recovery efforts, strapping down cargo and bailing water.

"Let's head to that shore of the island," proposed Davian.

"Yes, sir," replied the captain. "Raise the sails, men!"

As they prepared to set sail, BANG! A tremendous thud shook the ship. The sound echoed throughout the vessel, frightening the entire crew. Then, BANG, it happened again.

"What the hell is that!?" yelled the startled captain.

"Don't worry," replied Davian. "It's just the remaining waves settling down."

"Those aren't waves!" the captain cried in response. BANG! BAANNG! CRUUUNCH!

"What's going on!?" screamed a shipmate, hanging onto the ship's mast for support. The whole vessel was shaking.

"Did you run the ship aground?" asked Davian.

"No! We haven't hit any crags here," the sailor replied. "Something is hitting us from below!"

The ship lurched forward and backwards with the next wallop and several crewmembers carefully looked over the side of the ship to try to find the cause of the unnatural rocking. Just then, the banging stopped for a moment. They all braced themselves fearfully, expecting another strike to shake them, but nothing happened.

And just as the crew caught their breath enough to get back to minding the ship, the entire bow lifted up a dozen feet out of the water, forcing everyone—Davian included—to fall backwards towards the stern.

Out of the water emerged something the men had never seen before. It was a huge, multi-legged creature. There were so many writhing limbs that they couldn't count how many there were. No one had the time to even try to count anyways, as five of the massive tentacles gripped the bow of the ship. They were fat reddish appendages, each at least three feet thick, and lined with powerful suction cups and razor-sharp claws.

As the humongous sea creature continued to engulf the ship with its tentacles, two crewmembers grabbed swords and began to furiously chop at the slimy arms. Davian also pulled out a long sword and brought the weapon down upon one of the creature's limbs. As he swung, Davian's long robes opened to expose his dark glittering jewelry and fitted armor hidden beneath.

The sword, kept meticulously ever sharp, sliced open the thick tentacle, exposing the smooth white flesh inside and yellow fluid bled freely from the wound. Quickly, Davian pulled back for another strike and cleft the whole appendage cleanly in two. The severed tentacle squirmed angrily for a few seconds before stilling in defeat. Davian did not have long to rejoice over his victory, however, as another arm appeared from out of nowhere and wrapped itself around his sword.

Davian attempted to wrestle his sword from the creature. He wrenched the blade, twisting it in the monster's grasp, cutting into its skin and making it let go in pain. But as soon as he was able to retrieve the sword, yet another arm slithered onboard, swiping at Davian. By now, three sailors had already been pulled off ship and plunged into the churning depths beneath. Screams of horror echoed all around, and more slimy limbs kept appearing.

"We must fall back!" The captain shouted for the sails to be turned and attempted to steer the ship away from the creature.

No matter how much Davian and the others hacked at the beast's limbs, they would quickly heal and regrow, making their attacks almost useless. Slowly but surely, the sea creature began to overwhelm the ship.

All of a sudden, the deck of the ship was pulled almost equal to the water's surface. An extraordinarily large monster rose from the cyclonic depths below. Its mottled ruddy body was now in plain view, and everyone could see its terrible open maw.

Its enormous mouth was flanked by a gnashing beak lined with three layers of stark white fangs. The body was like an elongated tapered tube with flapping fins. Its huge cold eyes rested on either side of the body and the entire length of the arms could now be seen. They appeared to be about forty feet in length, not even including the rest of its body.

Understanding the peril they were all in, Davian dropped his sword onto the deck, raised his hands towards the creature, and uttered his secret words. Fearful of getting too close to the creature, a couple of sailors shot arrows into the tentacles from behind Davian, but they did little damage. The creature emitted an awful screech, as the arrows only served to anger it further, like putting splinters into a giant's finger.

Davian kept one of his hands raised while he pulled out a wand from within his robes. It started to glow blue as he spoke. Suddenly, a blue light flew from the tip, headed straight towards the creature's growling mouth. Seeing the glowing missile coming, it took one of its tentacles and swung at the light. The ball of light singed its arm where it hit, but the rest bounced from its slimy body, back to the boat, making a small smoky crater in the wooden deck. It was clear that the creature was truly formidable.

Now fully aware of its adversary, the creature focused its attention solely on Davian.

CHAPTER SEVENTEEN: A BROTHER IN NEED

"So, eh, yer lookin' fer work?" the young man asked while holding his drink in hand. His green eyes glittered curiously at them as he spoke in his own thickly accented voice.

Keeri returned with their food just as Unni was about to respond. "I thought you might want to eat it here instead," she said helpfully.

"Thank you," replied Unni as she placed the whole roasted chicken on the table in front of the dwarves.

"Please eat," the man urged. "We can all talk while we drink 'n dine, eh?"

Both dwarves nod in agreement.

"Did you want to order anything to eat?" Keeri asked the man.

"Ehh, no thank you, miss," he declined. "Eh've already eaten."

Unni and Okin didn't waste time diving into their meal. They tore into the roast chicken with gusto. It even came with sides of boiled carrots, potatoes, and barley. They showed no concern for manners or cleanliness as they scarfed down the food, crunching on the bones and all. They were used to eating so messily since they were almost always on the road traveling. Unni only realized how much food had fallen onto the floor as the others in the room began to eye their table.

Somewhat embarrassed, Unni motioned to Okin to show a bit more etiquette. "We're in public," he whispered.

Okin showed that he acknowledged his brother by slowing his food consumption.

The strange man laughed and introduced himself. "Meh name is Danelo and I'm from the city of Elgoshum en th'land eh Gueter. I need eh party t'find something important t'me."

He stroked his square chin as he talked. Unni and Okin tried to start eating more quietly, chewing slowly with their mouths closed, so as not to interrupt their client's story.

"What ya need us ta find for ya?" Unni asked, after swallowing a bite of his drumstick.

"Fren', lemmeh tell you how this all started, eh?" He smiled to them sadly and began. "Many years ago me 'n meh older brother were out exploring th'woods near our house. We knew it could be dangerous, but we were careless that day; We were jes' boys. We thought it'd be okay because it was so close t'home.

"Eh, anyway, we were jes' out walking when all of eh sudden, from th'bushes to th'left, we were tackled to th'ground! Eh group eh bandits grabbed us both. They were too many of 'em 'n they were too strong." Danelo explained bitterly.

"Coward tricks," Okin huffed.

"Yeh, coward indeed," Danelo agreed with a nod, his breath sounding short from emotion. "They boun' us up. Tied up our han's and dragged us t'their hideout. Their leader was there, yellin' orders at 'em all. He musteh been six feet tall 'n wearin' eh black 'n silver cigamian cloak. But that wasn't th' real surprise..." Danelo trailed off. "Th'wors' thing was... meh father 'n mother were there too."

Unni and Okin listened intently. Curious with where the story was going, they hadn't finished their food yet, but their eating wound down almost to a stop.

"What happened? Why was-ah your father there?" asked Unni.

"I'll get t'that," Danelo replied. "They put us in another room. There was a lotteh shouting though. We heard 'em yellin' at our paren's. When th'bandits would leave th'room to check on th'others, meh brother 'n I would struggle in our ropes. They were getting' looser little by little.

"We heard terrible things while we were tied up. Our mother was screamin'. She was sayin' stuff like, 'No, don't tell him!' And we could hear 'em beatin' her and yellin' at her t'shut up." His shining green eyes narrowed angrily above his long hooked nose as he thought of the brutes hurting his frail helpless mother.

"After eh while, we heard our father say, 'Stop, please don't hurt her again! I'll tell yeh everything! Please promise me that yeh won't hurt meh boys either.'

"Th'voice said t'him, 'Yer in no position to make demands.' It was th'leader, his voice all raspy like eh demon."

"Then what-ah happened?" asked the wide-eyed Unni.

"I was able t'twist out meh ropes. Meh brother couldn't. I tried t'help him get free, but..." Danelo's face fell as he tried to continue his tale. "Ehh..." he sighed and took a sip of his beer.

Unni and Okin looked at each other in shock. They hadn't been expecting a story like this.

"Meh brother begged me t'help him, but th'men were comin' back. I promised to find him someday. I was the only one that got away... But I intend t'keep meh promise..." His eyes seemed far away, looking at something only he could see—something from that terrible day burned into his memory.

"Ya want us ta help ya find-ah your family, then?" Okin said at last.

"No, jes' my brother. Meh parents were killed by 'em. They died terrible; they died brave. Meh brother was only kep' alive b'cause there's eh custom that the father passes his knowledge t'his eldest son first, 'n they didn't get all th'answers they needed from meh father b'fore slaying him."

They had been sitting, listening to Danelo's story for at least a half an hour before Keeri arrived at the table again. "Anything else to drink or eat?" she asked.

"Yes," replied Unni. Okin just nodded and pushed his empty mug towards her.

"I'll get eh refill too, miss," added Danelo.

"Good appetite, boys!" Keeri chirped as she gathered their empty plates and returned to the bar to retrieve their refills. She filled up all their mugs with a sweet smile and headed off.

Danelo watched her go and then said to the dwarves, "Well... That's meh story."

"That's an awful-ah tale," said Unni in condolence, his brother nodding. "Who was it who killed-ah ya parents?"

"His name is Davian," he stated darkly. "You help me

find him, 'n I'll find meh brother too."

"Davian, ah? Why does he still-ah have ya brother after all these years? What's ya brother know?" Okin questioned.

"Davian is lookin' fer dragons."

"Dragons!?" exclaimed Okin and Unni.

"Shhhh!" Danelo surveyed the room to make sure that no one was looking at them. "There is eh place where they're supposed t'live. My father told me too."

"Aren't-ah dragons just-ah myths?" asked Unni.

"Maybe. No one has ever foun' one 'n lived to tell the tale," said Danelo. "But will yeh help me find meh brother?"

Okin rubbed his bushy beard. "Sounds-ah dangerous. What's tha transport and-ah pay?"

"I'll provide you with th'boat fer transportation. Yeh can even keep it when we're done. Won't need it afterwards. As fer pay, Davian's bandits make like thieves with their lootin'. Yeh can keep all th'booty yeh find. Also, I can pay yeh two handsomely afterwards. I jes' want my brother back."

The dwarves looked at each other, communicating without words, while Danelo looked on with his hard emerald eyes. They both reached the same conclusion at the same time and nodded in agreement.

"Okay, we'll do it," declared Unni.

Danelo's eyes widened with surprise and relief upon hearing him. "That's great! I've asked many adventurers, but they all give up when I mention Davian's name. I knew yeh were different!"

"One-ah more condition," added Okin.

"What?"

"That-ah we can bring another person," finished Unni.

"Of course! Who's this mystery warrior?" asked Danelo.

"He's-ah one of our party," replied Okin. "He was-ah busy today, so we're getting-ah food here."

"We have an agreement?" asked Unni.

"Yeh, of course!" said Danelo enthusastically. "Let's meet at the double bald spot fork 'bout two miles south eh here. You'll know it when yeh see th'two grey stone circles b'fore th'intersection. Let's meet at dawn t'morrow," he suggested.

"Okay, Danelo," agreed the dwarves.

Danelo rose from the table, towering well above the dwarves, and headed out the door. A few heads turned his direction, almost as if they heard the conversation or sensed something strange about him.

"That's weird, brother," commented Okin in dwarvish.

Unni glanced at him. "What?"

"A bunch of people turned to watch when Danelo left the tavern."

"Maybe he was talking too loudly?" suggested Unni. "Anyway, let's tell Lorenz that we got us a job."

"Yeah, let's go," agreed the other dwarf.

They slid out of their oversized chairs and gathered up their gear. They strapped on their packs of supplies and fastened their weapons, Unni tucking away his bow and quiver of arrows, and Okin securing his axe in his belt.

"Oh, I forgot!" said Unni as he stopped in mid-stride. "We didn't pay for the meal."

"We don't have to," replied Okin, gesturing to the table. "Danelo already paid. Look."

Unni looked back at the table and saw the pile of fifteen gold coins sitting by his once again empty mug. There was enough money to pay for all of their food and drinks, and still leave a very nice tip for Keeri.

"That guy must be loaded," concluded Unni. "Perhaps this client is our big break," he added optimistically.

As the two made their way to the door, they did not notice as a certain set of eyes, which had been watching Danelo, followed them as they exited.

CHAPTER EIGHTEEN: LIGHTNING STRIKES

In the backyard, Lorenz gathered all of the ingredients for his spells. Most of them turned out to be relatively easy for him to find. He had a natural knack for reading the descriptions of the plants and identifying them, using the shape, contours and colors of the leaves, stems and roots. He had the hardest time with coal leaf, as it grew beneath the surface of the ground, leaving only a dark stem to sit above ground which camouflaged with the earth.

He rose after gathering the last ingredient when he heard: "It looks like you have gathered all of the ingredients you need."

Lorenz turned to face Thiek, and replied, "Yes. So, according to the book, I need to meditate briefly to be able to perform the spells. How long is a brief meditation period?"

"These spells require at least two hours of undisturbed mediation each at your level," he replied. "Remember, the better your focus, the less time it requires."

"Alright!" said Lorenz enthusiastically. "Let's go over there," he added and pointed.

To his left, about fifteen yards away was a small patch of reddish-orange grass and weeds. In the middle of this ochre meadow was a full-bodied tree, ripe with ruddy figs and heavy with shady leaves. The leaves, also red and orange like the grass below, were large and numerous, suspended by spindly, prickly branches. It looked like a pleasant place to sit. Within moments, Lorenz and Thiek reached the patch.

"Which spell do you want to try next?" asked Thiek after sitting down and making himself comfortable on the grass.

Lorenz was mostly excited about the lightning spell he'd seen in the book. A bit flashy and dramatic, but it was the truth.

Thiek smiled at him mischievously. "Let's do it."

Lorenz paused for a long time silently, visualizing a lightning bolt striking a clump of clovers several feet in front of him. He wasn't sure when he should stop, but gradually he felt a coolness overtake the air around him. He opened his eyes and looked up into the sky, momentarily removing his eyes from the weeds.

He noticed a small grey cloud quickly developing about high up in the air above them. Knowing he wasn't done yet, Lorenz then retrained his gaze on the patch of plants. He pointed his wand and a bolt of lightning struck immediately where he aimed—only it came from the tip of his wand. Not from the cloud in the sky as he'd imagined.

The incredible white-blue bolt struck ground and Lorenz's eyes widened in amazement. Never had he seen anything like this, especially at such a close range. He could even feel the hairs on his neck and arms tingle with electricity.

All the beautiful reddish-orange and green colors turned black before his eyes, burnt and obliterated by the hot lightning bolt. The grassy weeds burned and caught fire, quickly spreading to the brush and trees around as well, which alarmed Lorenz. He hadn't meant for the damage to spread.

Immediately, Thiek took out his wand, whispered something Lorenz could not make out, and flicked the tip of his wand towards the burning plants. A soft green flash of color came from the wand and settled over the charred black remnants of his garden plants. When the light finally dissipated a few seconds later, the singed black wasteland had been replaced with fresh green and red foliage once again. Lorenz was totally speechless at what he just seen.

"This is the power cigam?" he wondered to himself. "Unbelievable!" Thiek had just revived countless dead and withered plants. They looked fresh and vibrant as if nothing has ever happened to them.

Thiek just smiled. "You are going to be a marvelous talent," he commended.

Lorenz rubbed the back of his head in slight embarrassment. He hadn't meant for the lightning to get so out of hand. He didn't expect it to come out of his wand either.

"With cigam, things can happen differently than you might expect," replied Thiek.

"We must have some sort of inner connection," Lorenz finally said aloud. "You always seem to know what I'm thinking."

"When you have been practicing cigam for as long as I have, you develop a natural ability to communicate in various forms. Only those who are truly gifted in the ways of cigam possess this skill. One day soon, we will practice. I know that you have the ability, yet we still need to sharpen your skills—particularly how you hear others' hearts."

Lorenz nodded. Being able to read minds would blow his mind. It was like being a real live psychic. He knelt down and touched the place where the lightning had struck only minutes before, feeling the soft, cool blades of grass and clover.

After few more moments, Thiek suggested they do another spell. "Let's do one that is a bit tougher now."

CHAPTER NINETEEN: THE KILLER'S TRAIL

Now at the entrance of the big tavern, Ashawa, Dingle paused to survey the large dining area. Within seconds, most in the tavern noticed and recognized him. After a quick glance, they returned to their conversations and drinks.

"Sheriff!" called the server. He wore an apron with the name "Bran" stitched into the top pocket. "Uh, can I get you something, Sheriff?"

"Yeah, a glass of pale ale," answered Dingle. "Thank you, Bran."

A few moments later, the server brought Dingle's drink.

"Here you go, Sheriff," he said. "It's a good brew this time. Really smooth, just the right amount of sweetness and quality hops. I hope you enjoy it."

Dingle took a deep sniff of the frothy drink and then gulped a fourth of it down. "Yeah, it is a good batch. I'll have to come again later, when I'm not on duty."

"That's not all you're here for though?" inquired the server.

"You're right. Can you can tell me if anyone has seen a young male human traveler of average build around here last week? He was new in town. Leather armor and possibly dark skin and short hair."

"I think I know who you're talking about," Bran replied. "That person you're looking for did come in here about a week ago. Poor fellow. He left with that bastard, Jbug. Being that I haven't seen him or his goons lately, I can only hope he's dead by now."

"How did you know he's dead?" asked Dingle.

"I didn't know. I only *hoped*," Bran said bitterly. "If that person took care of him, all the better. Jbug got what was coming to him."

"Do you think you should talk about one of your late regulars that way? I don't know if that's very professional," commented Dingle a bit sharply. He was getting frustrated at how everyone kept cheering for his murder suspect.

Bran suddenly looked annoyed at the remark. "I'll tell you what's not 'professional,' Sheriff: the fact that the cops let beasts like him and his boys roam free in the streets. His gang only posed as 'regulars' in order to use our business place as his own personal hunting grounds. We didn't want the likes of him here, but we didn't wanna get on his bad side either, so we looked the other way. He was a monster, Sheriff. A damn monster. I bet you can't even guess how many he's robbed or killed."

"Just tell me what you know," he replied flatly.

The server just frowned at him. "Are you serious? You want to arrest the one who finally got rid of the town scum?"

"I'm very serious. What other information do you have?" continued Dingle, undeterred by Bran's attitude.

Bran rolled his eyes and sighed. "I got nothing then, Sheriff. The dark stranger came in, got some ale, and sat down. I never seen him before; he was just a traveler. Then that scumbag came and sat down next to him. Jbug always could smell the fresh meat. They chatted for a while, then left together. That's all I know."

"I see."

"Would you like anything else?" asked Bran in impatience. "Otherwise, I really have to get back to my work."

"No," replied Dingle. "Thanks for your help."

He turned to face the other tavern tables and a few looked back at him. They were no doubt wondering what business the town sheriff had with Ashawa. He left the building and once outside, he stood on the porch overlooking the main road. He watched the people walking by in the warm late afternoon as if in a trance. If what everyone said was true, all these men, women and children were safer with Jbug gone.

"Do I go after the one who stopped that parasite?" he asked himself. He know it was likely that the culprit only killed Jbug and his accomplices out of self-defense. Yet it was his duty to stop and catch criminals.

If things went down like Bran stated, the dark one came into the tavern alone and didn't know anyone there since he was a traveler, so Jbug probably tried to take advantage of him. Jbug likely made a bad move in the house and the man got the upper hand.

"I still need to meet him. I have to be able to talk to him to figure out if it was self-defense. I just have to make sure. After that, maybe I can even thank him for ridding us of Jbug."

The police had never been able to touch Jbug and his goons because the men always had alibis or there was never enough evidence to prove that they'd done anything. Bodies were never found and the few search warrants the police force had been able to acquire to inspect their hideout turned up nothing conclusive. Having someone outside of the law clean the problem up was almost a gift, though Dingle didn't approve of such actions.

"Now, the question is, where did this young man disappear to?"

He decided to make a quick trip south to the next town over to do some basic investigating.

CHAPTER TWENTY: REUNION

Thoroughly excited about performing his next spell, Lorenz hurried to gather the ingredients when that familiar dizzy feeling came about.

"No, not now!" whined Lorenz. "I'm about to do something!"

But it was to no avail. The spinning started even before he finished his last word. Very little time passed before he felt his feet on solid ground again. His eyes were blurry for a moment and soon, he recognized that he was in a great hall.

It had impeccable marble floors and richly carved wooden wainscoting. The walls were decorated with large original paintings of various types. A few were of landscapes or historic-looking buildings, but most of the paintings were of men in white curled wigs. Some depicted them engaged in meetings or speaking before large groups of people. Before Lorenzo was a large cherry wood door with a shiny golden knob.

"Is this real gold?" he wondered.

The entire place was simply lavish and amazing. Then, he realized he was in some sort of office building.

"Oh," he said to himself. And then it came to him. "This must be the Senate building! I'm working as an intern here on the weekends for my Government class." He couldn't believe that he was able to come here to work and get credit for his class. It was a great opportunity for work experience.

He decided he had better get inside a room, so Lorenzo turned the knob and saw an executive desk covered with papers and files. Behind it sat a woman.

The gilded rectangular desk lamp cast an odd greenish light on her and her sky-blue dress. She was in her twenties with pulled back blond hair and sharp blue eyes. She immediately looked up from the papers she'd been reading and before he even had a chance to enter, she asked, "Can you please take this to the secretary's office?"

She reached to her right and picked up a light brown folder and handed it to Lorenzo. "Take the underground route; it'll be faster. Thanks."

He nodded politely and took the folder from her with both hands and left the room. Then Lorenzo walked down the hall until he found some quartz-studded marble steps that wound downstairs. The walls here too were adorned with pictures in thick gilt frames. The stone balustrade along the stairs had an incredibly detailed floral design which he admired as he ran his hand along the carved banister and balusters.

Lorenzo walked down two flights of stairs which opened up to a large atrium. To his right, he found a sign with an arrow that indicated "Underground," lit by an incredibly beautiful crystal chandelier.

"I'd better keep going," he told himself. The sign indicated that he still had to descend to a lower level.

He kept to the right, down two more flights of stairs until he reached the basement. Here was a garage where numerous people were waiting for rides, and here was also the small open-air shuttle he needed. Lorenzo waited in line and started to board the vehicle when the spinning sensation washed over him once again.

"You have to got to be kidding me!" he grumbled silently to himself. "Why does it seem like every time I'm about to experience something interesting, I get interrupted?"

Within moments, he found himself standing beside Thiek in front of a wooden bench in the garden. At first, the bench was still, as expected. Then, it begins to quiver and its four legs started to lift up from the ground one at a time, taking turns rising and stepping about, as if it were dancing. It rocked left and right and crawled around the garden like a big curious dog. At one point, it even jumped into the air in joy. And the entire time, Thiek watched it and never flinched.

Lorenz was flabbergasted. Aside from a few electronic reclining chairs, like at the dentist, he had never seen a piece of furniture actually move, much less dance. The wood that the bench was made of was literally flexible, bending and twisting like human limbs. He was so amused and stunned by the sight that he almost forgot what spell he was practicing. He had to deanimate the animated bench.

"Alright," said Thiek. "The show's over. Take care of it."

So Lorenz pointed his wand in the direction of the bench and said the chant as stated in the book. As he finished, a hazy grey light filled with little spinning crystals materialized and shot from the tip of his wand and encompassed the bench in a sphere. Presently on two legs, the bench bent forward as if to bow, then stopped moving altogether. The crystals, still dancing and spinning, increased their speed. As they did, the bench seems to straighten out as if it were being ironed and the elevated legs lowered to the ground. It now sat as if it had never moved. The crystals dissipated, and all returned to normal. Lorenz was speechless.

In such a short period of time, he'd witnessed the most amazing transformation. A completely inanimate object had come to life and then he had taken the life back out of it. This was just a beginner's spell too. He could only imagine what more powerful spells would be like.

"I agree," replied Thiek. Then suddenly the old man straightened up and turned his head towards the house. "We have company."

Unni and Okin had reached Thiek's house where they last saw Lorenz last evening. The sun began to set quickly over the horizon once again, marking a full day's passage.

Thiek could sense them as after his experience with Jbug, Thiek had created a security system around his property to alert him of any visitors. "Someone is on the property, walking up the path," he said to Lorenz. "I believe they are friends of yours. Let's go and see who it is."

Following his teacher, Lorenz entered the house and headed into the bizarre, but still elaborately decorated living room. Multi-colored rugs and eerily smiling busts greeted him as he walked through the room. It had a wacky sense of design as far as he was concerned, but there was no doubt that the furniture and decor was nonetheless valuable and carefully selected.

They could hear knocking on the front door as they approached.

"Just a moment!" called Thiek.

As the dwarves heard the shuffling footsteps coming towards them and an old man's voice asking them to hold on. Okin looked at the bottom of the door and saw the feet of the one opening the door. They were in narrow purple slippers adorned with gold stars. He smirked to himself wondering what kind of person it could be.

Thiek undid the lock and let the two dwarves in. Lorenz recognized him immediately as his traveling partners. Thiek and the dwarves introduced themselves to each other.

When they were done, Lorenz stepped forward and greeted the dwarves warmly with a handshake. "Hey, glad to see you again! What's going on?"

"We gotta job! Someone hired us ta look-ah for someone. He will-ah be leading-ah the search," explained Unni, the slightly shorter dwarf brother, with a grin on his face.

"Where is the search taking place?" asked Thiek.

"We don't-ah know yet exactly," replied Okin.

"I would imagine it'd lead over some challenging trails," said Thiek.

"How do you know?" Lorenz asked the old mentor.

"A reasonable assumption given that the client hasn't yet specified the location," he replied. "Plus, I just have a feeling..."

"He didn't-ah tell us where we're going tah yet. Just-ah that he'd lead and tha' the reward is good," added Okin.

"I'm sure you'll be fine as long as all three of you stick together," assured Thiek, winking at Lorenz.

Lorenz smiled, seeing that his mentor was letting him postpone the lessons to go on the trip with his companions. "When and where are we going to meet him?" he asked.

"We're tah meet at dawn at the bald-ah fork in tha' road," said Okin.

"Alright, sounds good," replied Lorenz excitedly. "I think I'm ready for a challenge." Then turning to Thiek, he asked,

"Do you think I'm ready?"

"I think you will be fine as long as you remember the things we have discussed. The obstacles you will face will be different than the ones you have dealt with in the past. All of you must be prepared to tackle more difficult challenges and trust to each other."

By now, Thiek had led the group to be seated comfortably in the living room, where they listened to the old man talk.

"I am not sure about who your guide is, yet I believe that he will be a strong support. He will be someone you can trust," stated Thiek. "Now, enough listening to me go on. You all need to make your preparations. And a big part of being prepared for a journey is a proper meal. It's now late. Why don't I fix us all dinner?" he offered.

"Ya, I'm-ah hungry," replied Okin.

Unni rolled his eyes at his brother. "We just ate at-ah the Cove!"

Okin just laughed. "I'm-ah bigger. I need-ah to eat-ah more!"

Unni shook his head. "Thank you for-ah your offer."

"Make yourselves at home."

"I'm so excited to have you guys at dinner at my teacher's home," said Lorenz. "I'm glad that you got to meet one another."

"Ya," Okin and Unni agreed.

"Wait, Thiek, do you want me to help you prepare dinner?" Lorenz asked.

The old man shook his head gently. "You three sit and chat," Thiek said. "I'm sure Unni and Okin have some valuable information to share with you."

"Thanks so much-ah sir," replied Unni.

"Sir?" laughed Thiek. "I'm not that old! At least not yet." He let out a hearty guffaw and headed into the kitchen.

Once he entered the kitchen and closed the door, Okin turned to Lorenz and Unni. "He is a wise and kind-ah man."

"Yeah, he is," agreed Lorenz. "I always wondered how he knew so much, but at least it cuts down on me asking too many stupid questions," he joked.

Okin and Unni spent a few minutes admiring the plush furnishing and fine art in the living room. As rough and tumble travelers, they never had any chances to visit such luxurious homes before.

Thiek soon returned to the living room with a tray of drinks. "Ale?" he offered. "I brewed it myself from the barley in my garden out back."

"Thanks," said Lorenz as he passed the glass to his friends and kept one for himself.

Thiek hummed happily and turned around with the empty tray to head back to the kitchen.

"So, what's the story with the client?" asked Lorenz finally.

"So, here's tha deal," starts Unni. "This man-ah named-ah Danelo, his brother Danilo was kidnapped-ah by Davian some-ah years ago. Davian came-ah ta his house and murdered his parents."

Lorenz took a careful sip of his drink. "Only he escaped?"

"Ya. He's been tryin' and searchin' for a long-ah time for his brother," replied Okin.

"Does he know where Davian took his brother?"

"He didn't-ah say specifically."

"I've heard that Davian is a dangerous man who's out to get one thing in particular," continued Lorenz.

"What?" asked Unni.

"Dragons," stated Lorenz.

"Dragons," echoed Okin. "Tha's what-ah Danelo said ta us too."

"Yeah, supposedly if he gets one, he'll be pretty much unstoppable," added Lorenz.

"We understand," stated Okin. "Dragons are said ta be much more strong-ah than ya average monster."

"If we're looking for Davian's captive, it will be a dangerous journey," said Lorenz.

Just then, Thiek came back into the room.

"Dinner is ready".

CHAPTER TWENTY-ONE: LIGHTNING STRIKES AGAIN

Davian could barely stand straight as the ship tilted in the monster's grasp. He glared at the creature that now stared back at him with hollow beastly eyes. Focused on protecting the ship, he quietly uttered a spell. As the creature continued to take over the boat, almost like a toy in its arms, its probing tentacles found and pulled two hapless sailors overboard.

The men unfortunate enough to be pulled or thrown overboard were tossed like ragdolls in the batting of the waves. The monster's thick tentacles wrapped around their waists, squeezing them tight, forcing the air from their lungs. It was unclear if they died from being crushed by the constricting arms or if they drowned first, but their faces twisted in horrible agony as the men onboard watched them piteously.

Concentrating intensely, Davian looked into the creature's eyes and furrowed his brows. Within moments, the skies that had been relatively clear suddenly grew dark with clouds. They were thick, intense, and dangerous. The clouds themselves seemed to buzz with raw energy.

As the grey mass continued to gather above them, the boat groaned and cracked loudly under the dangerous pressure of the fiend. It struggled to stay afloat while the men continued their frantic efforts to stop the creature.

Below the deck, all that had been neatly stored was now in disarray. Luggage, crates of food, barrels of ale, and boxes of supplies were strewn everywhere. With this cargo was also a certain young man who was said to know where the dragons dwelled. And above, Davian maintained his concentration despite all the chaos.

Just then, a stark blue lightning bolt blasted out from the clouds and struck the creature right in its wide, unblinking eye. The smell of cooked flesh and a blood-curdling screech filled the air. Nursing its wound, the beast slowly let go of the ship and slunk back into the water. Salty and soaking wet from a mixture of sweat and seawater, the men cheered.

A smirk crept across Davian's face as he yelled for the captain to steer the ship away.

"Yes, sir!" he replied and ran for the wheel.

CHAPTER TWENTY-TWO: THE NIGHT BEFORE

A few hours into the evening, after much feasting and talking, the two dwarves and humans were still sitting at the long wooden table while their dirty plates, mugs, and silverware rose up and made their way to the sink. Never having dined with a cigamian before, Unni and Okin stared in amazement at this feat.

"I recommend you gentleman prepare for bed," suggested Thiek. "You will need every bit of your rest. The journey ahead is no easy one. Should you face Davian, what tricks of mine you just saw here at dinnertime are nothing compared to the cigam you will see him use."

"He sounds fearsome," Unni agreed.

"If you two are ready, I will show you to your room where you can stay for the night," Thiek offered while rising.

He led them back through the living room and up a spiral flight of stairs. It was quite dark now that it was night and the only sources of light were the ornate candelabras lining the walls of the hallways they walked.

The turn for Lorenz's room was first, so he told Thiek and the dwarves good night. "See you guys in the morning. I'm right here if you need anything." And with that, he disappeared down the steps into his room.

Next, Thiek escorted Unni and Okin to their bedroom for the evening. Though he waved them in, Unni paused at the door and quickly scanned the chamber.

Reading his uneasiness, Thiek replied, "It's safe. But please feel free to check it out first, if you like."

So, Okin entered after Unni and both brothers looked it over. Inside the cream-colored room were two massive beds positioned perpendicular to each other. The beds must have been a dozen feet long by a half dozen feet wide. A giant could have slept on them! The mattresses were thick and high from the ground, perched on a golden frame. It was a very entreating sight for tired travelers of any sort. On the floor next to each bed, the dwarves noticed a small stool for them to use to be able to climb into them.

The room also held several bookshelves for reading to pass the time, and several high-backed chairs or a long white oak bench to sit in whilst reading. There also was a large vanity mirror as well as a couple of chests of clean clothes, linens and towels.

"Wow," whispered Okin. "This is a very nice-ah room."

"It-ah looks perfect, Thiek. Thank you for-ah ya hospitality!" Unni said warmly to express his gratitude.

"You're welcome, my friends, and good night," said Thiek. After giving them a nod and a warm smile, he closed the door for their privacy, and returned to Lorenz's room back the way he came.

He found the young man organizing his belongings in preparation for the journey. He was placing changes of clothes and some sheets into his bag.

"So..." began Thiek from the threshold. "Are you ready?"

"Um, I'm not sure" he replied honestly. "Maybe? I think I am..."

"What about your spells?" Thiek continued as he leaned against the doorway entrance with his arms folded.

"Yeah," Lorenz said. "I definitely know the spells I studied with you."

"Why don't you pick a couple of similar level spells to learn while on your trip?" suggested Thiek.

"Alright."

"Well, it's time for bed, young man," Thiek said. "It is important for you to get your rest, or else you won't be able to focus your mind on your spells."

"Alright, I'll remember that."

"Good night then, lad." The teacher unfolded his arms and left, closing the door behind him.

Within a few minutes, Lorenz was dressed in comfortable sleepwear and ready for bed. As he pulled back the thick quilted blankets and crawled into bed, the candles in the room knew to snuff themselves out and he was able to quickly fall into a deep sleep.

CHAPTER TWENTY-THREE: THE STORM

The next morning started with a slight breeze and a brisk chill in the air. It was that time of the year when fall began to blend into winter. The trees were full of leaves turning into vibrant shades of yellow, orange, and red. The warmth of the colors cast a brilliant charm on the autumn air.

In Thiek's house, shades and star-spangled blinds kept out the light of slowly rising sun. Okin, Unni, and Lorenz lingered peacefully in slumber, wrapped up coxily in their blankets. Thiek, too, seemed to cling to the comfort of his bed, though against his will.

"It's time to rise," he told himself. "There is little dark left and they must depart soon."

He reached for his wand lying on the end table. With a quick small circular motion and a flick, a ball of light began to grow from the end of the wand. It split and formed into two circular objects that resemble two small fists balled up. They left Thiek's room quickly and flew through the air to the respective sleepers' doors. The glowing bronze fists rapped on Lorenz's and the dwarves' doors, shouting, "Wake up time!"

Inside his room, Lorenz stirred, turning over in hid bed to face the door. In a few moments, he remembered that he was in his room at Thiek's house. He sat up and pacified the magic fist with a groggy "uhh" in response. Okin and Unni, too, moaned at the early alarm, allowing the fist to dissipate from their door.

In a short period of time, all three men had washed up and ended up downstairs in the kitchen, still sleepy-eyed and yawning. They were rewarded by the sight of the dining table spread with fruits, goats' milk, and barley, oats and other grains. They each sat down at the places prepared for them as Thiek urged them saying, "Hurry; we do not have the luxury of a leisurely breakfast! Time is not on your side today."

Quickly, they all dug into the food with few words

and finished eating within a few minutes. Lorenz was just finishing his glass of milk and Okin was still sucking bits of blackberry seeds from his teeth when Thiek began to address them.

"Alright travelers, it is time," said Thiek.

"We're very thankful-ah for-ah ya hospitality," stated Unni again.

"Ya," agreed Okin.

"You are most welcome," replied their host.

Their gear was packed and waiting for them near the front door and they made ready to leave. Moments later, Unni opened the front door. A cold breeze and dark sky with minimal creeping golden light welcomed him. They each grabbed their bags and headed out the door.

Standing at the front entrance, Thiek stopped Lorenz and told him, "Remember everything we have studied together."

"Of course, Thiek."

The three comrades walked down the windy path leading back to the main road while the old mentor remained in the doorway, seeing them off as they went their way. Once they reached the road, Lorenz turned for a last good-bye wave. Thiek smiled, turned, and closed the door.

Unni, Okin and Lorenz all stopped together at the crossroads to discuss the plans.

"So, which way are we heading?" he asked the brothers.

"It's-ah this..." But before Unni could finish his sentence, Lorenz's hearing faded and he knew that he was being transported. He was irritated at the timing yet again, but there was nothing to be done about it. All the strenuous work and practicing cigam he'd been doing with Thiek had exhausted his spiritual energy, so he was fading in and out more frequently than before.

In a moment, the spinning stopped. When his vision cleared, he recognized the familiar red brick building and busy street.

"I'm at school."

He stood on the front steps of the school, facing the bookstore and café across the street. While looking around, he noticed the small white flakes falling from the sky.

"Gosh, it's cold," he mumbled and shivered. Lorenzo puffed some warm breath onto his icy hands and tightened the thick coat around his body.

He remembered that a few minutes ago—in this realm— he was sitting in his English classroom when the teacher told the class to head home early and stay indoors. School had been released due to a serious snowstorm warning; a blizzard was estimated to approach the area by that evening.

The snow was already falling more heavily just within the last few minutes he'd been walking to the bus stop. The ice was coming down thicker and the flakes were getting bigger. The wind was really starting to pick up as well—so much so that visibility had started to diminish. He squinted across the street, shading his eyes from the falling snow. The buildings and bus stop across the way could clearly be seen a few minutes before, but not anymore. He had better get indoors soon.

The stop was a couple of blocks away from the school, so he started in that direction, walking as briskly as he could. He and several other students reached the intersection that led to the bus stop and within a few minutes, the bus arrived as scheduled. They got on, but there were already no seats left to take. The vehicle carried at least fifty people, many of whom were standing and hanging onto the poles. The bus was especially crowded today because of the bad weather, but it was fine since Lorenzo only needed to ride it for a few stops. He hung onto a metal pole himself and brushed the snow from his coat.

The school bus was striped in red, white, and blue with a large windshield and big square windows where he could see the long windshield wipers trying weakly to clear the front window of ice. The snow was coming down much heavier and faster, causing the wipers to move awkwardly and out of synch as they swept through sheets of ice.

Lorenzo had ridden through about five stops and it had gotten so full that the bus driver couldn't even stop for anyone else. The next bus would have to pick up the other waiting people outside in a few minutes. During the route, the turns and stops started to feel more sloppy and jerky. Everyone could feel the bus losing traction on the road as more and more snow got packed onto the road. Braking was just plain scary. Many were afraid while the bus was moving and a couple of times, Lorenz thought they were going to skid into the intersection.

"Everyone off the bus," ordered the driver suddenly. It had gotten to the point where it was becoming too dangerous for the large vehicle to drive. Streets had accumulated at least five inches of snow and the heavy bus was skidding too much. Cars could drive with more ease than the huge bus could.

After getting off the bus with dozens of others, Lorenzo decided to walk the several blocks left to the next transit stop, but no driver would agree to take him or the others home. It was too dangerous for them to drive passengers with their clumsy vehicles. In fact, several buses were sitting on the side of the road with signs saying "out of service" or driving away at a snail's pace with no one else on board. All around him, other students complained and began calling their parents or other relatives to drive them home. Everything had been blanketed in white.

Lorenzo passed by a tall, old office building. It housed offices for department stores and had the subway underneath. Traffic everywhere moving very slow, but luckily there were only minor accidents. Fender benders at most.

Lorenzo's mother was busy working on the other side of town and he couldn't see any friends he recognized in the crowd of students, so he resolved to walk home.

"It shouldn't take more than forty minutes to walk, even with the snow," he thought.

He'd only been traveling for a couple of blocks when a different bus pulled up to a stop he was passing. According to the electronic display, this bus was still in service. Apparently this model was safer on slippery roads, with a shorter roof and wider wheels.

As soon as it stopped, Lorenzo was able to climb aboard with a mass of other shivering people. He reached in his pocket and pulled out the plastic pass card to show to the driver, though honestly, in this kind of weather, they wouldn't force people to pay for fare. He made his way towards the middle of the bus, finding again that all the seats had been taken. Lorenzo finally found a spot to stand in and held firmly onto the aluminum pole. He looked out the window at the monotonous snowbound scene until he was interrupted by the whining static of a radio.

Lorenz turned to look at the rear of the bus and saw a young man dressed in a black hoodie-jacket sitting with a small blue stereo on his lap. Just then, Lorenz jerked backwards as the engine of the bus revved and the vehicle started moving. He tightened his grip so he wouldn't fall over.

The man with the radio had turned it onto a news station. Lorenzo didn't know any of the people around him, so he decided to listen to the fellow's stereo to pass the time. On normal day, the bus ride only took about twenty minutes. Today, it already had been almost two hours.

"We have just received news that a large subway car had been derailed, swiping into another train. At least twenty-five people have been reported injured and there are still five people trapped inside the wrecked train car. There have been no fatalities in this accident, but several passengers are in critical condition."

Lorenzo winced. He was having a bad day, but those people were faring far worse than he was.

"A passenger plane has also been reported to have gone down into the Potomac, killing at least sixty passengers who were either killed on impact or frozen in the waters. This day is has proven to be one of the most tragic of our city's history."

Several other people who were listening to the news report exclaimed in shock and sympathy for the victims of the accidents. Lorenzo himself had been listening to the announcement so intently that he didn't even notice the buzzing sensation take over his body.

CHAPTER TWENTY-FOUR: THE FORK IN THE ROAD

His heart was still racing thinking about the plane's crash into the Potomac River. Lorenz kept thinking about the tragedies as he slipped back into place with Unni and Okin. He hoped nothing bad like that would happen here.

They were walking down the road with the sun having risen enough to slightly above the low cloud line, lighting up the sky in gold and pink. Up ahead he could see the road appear to split. There were two circular spots in the ground that measured about three feet in diameter. A man seemed to be waiting for them there.

"Here," pointed Okin. "He's tha client."

They reached the fork to find the hook-nosed Danelo. Lorenz, glancing over the solemn-looking man in silence, decided that he could indeed trust him. His gut told him so.

Danelo nodded his head to the three and greeted them. "Morning," he called.

"This's tha guy I was telling ya about," stated Unni.

He let Lorenz and Danelo introduce themselves to one another.

"So, eh are we ready?" the man asked his crew.

Lorenz nodded and shifted his backpack. "Yes, but where are we headed?"

"We're gonna head t'the south," he answered. "Did Unni 'n Okin fill yeh in on the mission?"

"I b'lieve he's southwest eh here," said Danelo. "Yeh see, our race, we have eh special way t'communicate with each other. We can sense where each other are. But th'signal is getting weaker. It's imperative that we fin' my brother as soon as possible."

Danelo turned to the pathway on his right and started walking. Lorenz and the dwarves immediately set off after Danelo in a single file line. Danelo was a tall man and his pace was quick, so every so often, he would look back to make sure that everyone was keeping up. Everything about him, his hard face and eyes, his fast wide strides, had a sense of urgency and concern. Before they knew it, they had walked about two miles.

The foliage of the trees around them was getting denser and the trees and shrubs were different from the ones near Thiek's house. The small party continued their trek with the sun trailing to the middle of the clear, blue sky. During the last mile, no other people had been spotted on the road.

Lorenz was puffing to keep up with Danelo, but the dwarves with their short legs were having an even harder time of it. The brothers were panting and constantly wiping sweat from their brow.

"Yeh feel like yeh need to take eh break?" asked Danelo finally.

"Ya, sure. Let's get-ah ta tha clearing up here," said Unni.

The men and dwarves enter reached the patch of flat ground and rested on the rocks and logs there. Lorenz took a flask of water from his bag and took a big, quenching drink. Okin fanned himself with a large leaf he plucked from a tree, sighing with exhaustion.

"Yeh hear that?" Danelo suddenly asked.

Everyone stopped what they were doing and listened. There was indeed a sound, a low growling and shuffling in the distance. But it was getting closer.

Lorenz put on his armor and he and Danelo both drew their swords. They scanned their surroundings for the source of the sound, but it was impossible to see anything through all the trees and plants. Unni had readied his bow and Okin was hanging onto his axe.

While the group waited to see if the intruder would approach, Danelo asked Lorenz what gifts he had to help in the fight.

"Well, I have an enchanted sword and armor and I know a little cigam" he replied.

"Good. We will need it," he said gravely.

Finally, they heard a mixture of heavy footsteps and something being dragged down the path.

"C'mon ya filthy beasts," whispered Okin as he readied his axe in hand.

Something big and scaly was lurking just beyond the trees in the distance. Peering closer, Unni announced, "It's still-ah coming. Maybe I can-ah shoot it with-ah my bow."

With incredible deftness, the dwarf aimed and shot his target, causing the creature to shriek in pain as the arrow clung in the beast's scaly hide. With a menacing growl, it lumbered toward the group angrily.

Lorenz, knowing a few spells by heart, began to concentrate.

The creature attempted to pull the arrow out of its body and made even more ruckus than before, but while the creature was tending to his injury, Unni quickly prepared to shoot another arrow at it. He pulled and let fly. The arrow whizzed just past the angry beast. Just then, something else came into view.

The creature, still furiously trying to pull out the arrow out, finally succeeded. Unfortunately, it was now joined by two beasts just like it. Their bodies were vaguely like that of a gorilla, except with longer snouts and thick crocodilian scales covering all their skin. The three advanced towards the party, holding spears, closing in on the distance that separated them.

"Yeh'd better stop where yeh are, unless yeh want more," Danelo warned. Plunging his sword into the ground, he immediately grabbed for his own bow. He swiftly brought his own arrow, which was much larger than Unni's weapons, back and shot. A second creature was hit and wailed in rage. It grabbed at the arrow, now lodged in its upper thigh, and tore it out. Thick reptilian blood begins to pour from the wound.

Okin and a monster each rushed towards one another. The dwarf planned to feint left, then attack from the right, hitting the creature in the leg. Meanwhile, Unni only had time for another arrow or two before he'd have to jump into the melee with his own blade.

A spear thrust towards Okin, but failed miserably. The giant blade glided through the air, passing Okin's left side by a wide margin as the dwarf dove towards the ground in a tuck and roll and successfully evaded the creature's assault.

A second fiend reached back with his weapon, preparing to stab at Okin, but the dwarf saw the motion and raised his axe in an attempt to strike first. The creature pulled back and blocked Okin's first blow. The axe's blade collided with the wood and metal spear, resulting in a resounding clang. Being smaller and faster, Okin recovered from the swing first and this time, he sliced into the upper-calf of the creature, shredding the layers of scales and muscle tissue in its leg.

The creature hurled its spear back at Okin, but missed. The wound in it leg caused too much pain for accuracy. The creature, now disabled and disarmed, was unable to defend itself, so Unni moved in for the kill.

The single creature still armed growled deeply as it brought its weapon towards Unni, who was trying to advance on its hurt partner. Unni decided he had to duck and roll under the blade and past the creature's legs.

While preparing to deal the first creature a final blow, Danelo prepared another arrow for a newly emerged fourth creature coming into view.

Lorenz's eyes widened as he said to himself, "This is almost too much to see! I've never had to deal with a battle like as this one." He knew that he couldn't just stand and watch; he needed to help. Yet his gut told him to wait a little longer for the opportunity to come.

Danelo released his next arrow that soared though the air towards the fourth creature. En route, it sped by Unni's left side and pierced the target's great mid-section. The creature screeched and glared at the wound.

Unni's small axe sliced through the incapacitated creature's right arm like a hot knife through butter. Meanwhile, his brother continues his assault on another.

Okin finished his creature by severing its head. It fell backwards with a messy, sickening thud. He saw Unni successfully evade another of the creatures while Danelo prepared to shoot another arrow from his vantage point on a boulder.

The armed creature battling with Unni hounded the small dwarf with endless stabs and parries and slashes. As Unni attempted to keep evading the monster, it finally managed to plunge its spear into his right boot.

Fortunately, it has struck towards the side and only cut the skin superficially. Unni flinched, grunting in pain, and he refocused his anger on striking the creature.

Lorenz watched all of this take place and was raring to fight. He took his sword, thinking, "I have to do something! I can't just stand here." However, his gut feeling told him to be patient.

He started to question it, but then remembered how badly it had done him to not heed it in the past. He bet Unni and Okin and Danelo were wondering why he was just standing there on the sidelines.

With incredible precision, Danelo's arrow struck one of the creatures in the head. It lodged itself between its eyes and in a flash, the six-foot tall creature fell forward like chopped tree. Once it hits the ground face first, the arrows blade pushed the rest of the way through the creature's skull for all to see.

But just as this creature hit the ground, three more appeared from behind the trees. It was never ending. They just kept coming. Ignoring the pain for the moment, with all his might, he Unni, reached back, striking a fresh lumbering creature in the back. It raised its head and screeched in agony as the hand axe, split the skin, slicing through scales. That one lunged for Unni and the other two headed for Okin. Overwhelmed, the dwarves had to begin falling back.

Seeing this, Lorenz prepared his sword. "Alright, here we go!" he whispered with trepidation.

And suddenly, one of them had its weapon aimed at

Lorenz's midsection and he prepared to block the attack when he felt the vibrating sensation begin again without warning.

At the worst possible moment, he was engulfed in the spinning...

CHAPTER TWENTY-FIVE: DWINDLING TIME

Dingle was having a hard time relaxing as the days went on and he kept wondering where the killer was. All his efforts now might be for naught. The killer could be in another country by now for all he knew.

With the sun high in the sky, he walked down the main road. Entering from one of the side trails was a petite woman with long grayish-black hair. She was startled by Dingle's sudden presence and jumped slightly. Dingle, startled as well, quickly turned to acknowledge the woman.

"Manerva, how are you?" he asked, relieved. It was just the cobbler's wife. "Heading into town to order more leather?"

The older woman smiled at him and fixed her lilac dress. "Why, yes. Such a detective you are, dear. How are you, Dingle? Finding enough time polish your shiny badge?" She joked with him openly, having known Dingle for many years.

"Actually, I've been occupied with looking for someone," he replied. "He's a dark man of average height who may have traveled this way about a week ago."

"A week ago, dear? Well, I have no news for you," she answered. "You may want to inquire at the house down the road there on the right. The old man there is usually home. He may have seen someone. Good day, Sheriff!" she concluded as she continued towards town.

He quietly watched her travel down the road for a bit, then looked towards the house she indicated. This place again...

The sun began to set on the horizon. Davian, frustrated, shouted, "I'll give you one day! I want that exact location including how to get around the bay!"

The half-Elvish man, bruised and cut, looked up through his undamaged eye at Davian. His swollen, split lips quivered as he tried to say, "I don't, eh, know..."

Davian backhanded him again and Danilo's face turned red at the impact and jerked to the right. His head drooped as he fell unconscious.

The spinning ceased and his vision cleared as Lorenzo found himself in a new place. All around him was darkness and something else he was not used to seeing—a hay wagon. Above, the sky was filled with incredibly large and bright stars. All he could do was stare up at them until he heard a voice say, "Lorenzo, let 's go."

And just as he turned to see who it was, the pull in his guts happened again and everything went black.

It had never happened this quickly to him before, and for a moment, he was worried. He did not have the time to ponder the quick transport however, as within moments, he was back in the battle.

Lorenz barely had the time to block the oncoming spear with his sword. The creature staggered back. Lorenz, seeing his advantage, raised his sword in one swift movement and brought it down on the creature's head.

The monster's skull split open, but the sword continues to slice down through it, dividing the body asunder. Its knees slammed hard to the ground and the creature knelt there for another second before it collapsed altogether.

Unfortunately, as Lorenz looked up, he saw a trail full of the same fiends headed in the direction of his party. Noticing the new beasts, Okin roared a bloodcurdling cry and without hesitation, ran to hack up one of the creatures with his axe like chopped pork. When the reinforcements appeared to behold the destruction of their brethren, their eyes widened in fear and they returned with tails tucked from whence they came.

Everyone at once give a sigh of relief and let their aching shoulders slump.

"We need t'continue movin'. Time is not on our side," Danelo stated. "No more breaks."

"What about seeing if-ah these things have anything of value?" suggested Okin.

"I can guarantee they have nothing worthwhile," assured the elf. "We oughta go before more decide t'show up."

"He's probably right," agreed Lorenz.

The group gathered their belongings and headed back towards the trail up the hills, with Unni limping from the wound in his foot.

"You okay, Unni?" Lorenz asked in concern.

"Ya, I'm fine," he grimaced. "It's not-ah too deep. I'm just-ah tired."

About an hour into the journey, Okin asked, "Are we gonna eat-ah soon?"

"Not right now," replied Danelo. "We need t'keep moving. Davian won't keep meh brother alive much longer if we don't fin' him soon. We'll rest in a few more miles."

They continued to walk and talk along the way for a long while until Lorenz stopped all of a sudden. Unni was fairly quiet during the conversation and limping pretty badly by now, but that wasn't what had halted him. There were rustling noises coming from the woods near them. He took a defensive position and stared out into the trees, at which point Lorenz noticed Unni stumble.

He immediately turned to catch the dwarf. "Danelo!" he shouted just loud enough for the elf—and whatever might be coming up behind them—to hear. He had to get Danelo and Okin to stop.

The two in the lead stopped and hurried back.

"What-ah happeneda?" Okin asked while shaking his head.

As Lorenz relaxed his hold on the injured dwarf, he saw the telltale trail of red drops along the trail. "He's been bleeding a lot."

"Do ya have a medicine kit?" Okin asked. "Unni, wake up," urged Okin, shaking his brother's limp shoulders.

Lorenz knew that he had to try to heal Unni, but there was that noise still. He cursed not having thought to check the dwarf over for his injuries before when they were free. Unni hadn't told them that the injury was so serious.

The blood was coming from Unni's foot. Lorenz quickly pulled off the dwarf's boot and then peeled the sticky sock soaked with blood from his foot. The injury wasn't terrible, but the blood loss mixed with the exhaustion of the fight and trying to keep up with the others had really done a number on him.

"You can do this," Lorenz told himself. He pulled out his wand and bwasan healing salve he'd made previously with Thiek. In a flash, he rubbed the herbal ointment onto the wound and uttered the incantation. Then he touched the injured foot with the wand and as he did, the bleeding slowed and stopped.

Unni stirred and started to open his eyes. Lorenz was relieved that Unni was all right, but readied himself for a fight. Okin and Danelo were of the same mindset.

"Get ready, you guys!" he told the dwarves. "Something's coming!"

Hearing this, Okin helped Unni get his boot back on and got to his feet. The once-wounded dwarf was feeling much better. With everything happening so fast, Lorenz had no time to marvel at what he had done for his friend. All he could think was: "Something is coming and we just finished fighting a couple hours ago!"

CHAPTER TWENTY-SIX: THE MISSING BROTHER

With luck, the sounds seemed to be a false alarm, as whatever was making them began to move away. The four continued on their way.

The path continued straight ahead for another twenty-five yards where it turned and inclined to the right and wound into the forest. It seemed to continue for miles and the trees alongside the trail gradually changed. They became larger and denser than they had been before and appeared to be changing their foliar raiment from bright fall colors to dull winter ones.

When they eventually came upon some fallen logs that looked like they'd make good seats, Danelo stopped the group, telling them it would be a decent place to take a short break to eat dinner.

"Sounds good," says Lorenz. "It'll be dark before long."

Everyone set up their own little place in which to eat. Lorenz and Danelo took opposite ends of a large log to rest their feet and the dwarves plopped themselves down on the ground, leaning against their tree logs. It did not take long for them all to finish their meals that they had packed. Soon, all that was left were some bread crumbs and fruit seeds scattered in the dirt.

"I felt like I hadn't eaten in a week. I didn't realize how hungry I was until I started eating—and that was pretty hungry!" Lorenz mused.

"Ya tellin' me," laughed Okin as he pat his belly.

Immediately after eating, they got back onto the road. As the trail wound higher and higher in elevation, there were numerous stone fixtures of various sizes, shapes and colors studded along the road. They were strange rounded carvings made long ago by some people for some reason. Lorenz wasn't sure what they were supposed to represent, but luckily no one and nothing came out to surprise them as they traveled through the area.

The sun was beginning to set and Lorenz's legs and feet

were aching, even in this plush boots. They'd been walking all day. He'd probably be really sore tomorrow. He'd never had to travel so much before or so quickly, but he knew he couldn't stop since another person's life was on the line.

"Let's jes' keep goin' a while longer," Danelo suddenly said, as if he could tell what Lorenz was thinking—which by now wouldn't have surprised him. "We'll stop fer the night when darkness falls. This area is a good place t'stop in any case. Right b'fore the bogs."

Lorenz saw what he meant. From their vantage point on the mountain, he could see in the distance below them a vast expanse of olive brown mud. Tall brown and green weeds mingled into the high dark grass and decorated the soggy marsh. Beyond these bogs were mountains with gigantic rock formations. Lorenz surmised that the water from the rains and snows must collect in stony basins in the valleys of these rocky mountain ranges, making huge areas of stagnant water and muddy soil.

"Meh brother is still alive," Danelo continued. "But jes' barely. However, if we keep moving quickly, I think we'll be able t'save him."

His green eyes stared forward gravely as usual, but this time, there was a small glimmer of hope in them.

"It's okay, Danelo," said Lorenz. "We can keep going, right guys?"

"Ya," Unni and Okin agreed.

"Let's keep going, past the bog. Let's find your brother. He's coming home soon," he declared.

Touched by the others' encouragement, Danelo tipped his wide-brimmed hat forward slightly and smiled.

The storage room Davian paced in was small, dank and dim. His boots clicked softly, but threateningly in the darkness. Closing the door with its worn metal handle, he was ready to interrogate his captive once again.

Inside this dark room was Danilo, Danelo's older brother, whom he had kidnapped years before. His body was scarred and emaciated from years of torture and starvation.

He hung his head against his chest weakly and his arms were tied with coarse metal chains. His whole body was such a pitiful sight; it was hard to tell what part of him was the worst. Lacerations covered his chest, arms, and back from cruel whips. He was missing several teeth and his nose was crooked from vicious beatings. Plus, his wrists were bruised, bleeding and calloused from his permanent bindings.

As Davian entered the room with a couple of men, the half-elf slowly raised his head a bit. With the brightness of daylight in his face, Danilo winced and closed his eyes.

"Eh, jes' kill meh 'n get it over with, please," he gasped. He was dizzy and could hardly stay conscious long enough to talk. His weakened body felt as if it was always fluttering between life and death, ready to expire. They were feeding him scraps only once a day or two now and beating him more and more. They were close to getting rid of him, he was sure.

"You have one more opportunity to make things better for yourself," stated Davian. "You know that if you just tell me, your suffering will end."

In a whisper, barely even audible, the elf said to him hoarsely, "I don' know..."

Heading into the expansive, slimy marshland, Danelo stopped in his tracks. He paused, lowering his head. Then without warning, his body jerked in a spasm and he gave a choked cry. They all stopped, realizing that he must be experiencing some type of immense pain.

"Is there anything I can do?" asked Lorenz.

"What's wrong-ah with him?" inquired Unni nervously.

"I think something is happening with his brother!"

With great intensity on his face, Danelo gritted his teeth and said, "We have t'hurry. We don't have much time. Danilo is fading!"

The man, still holding his head in pain, continued to lead them on the path to the marsh.

"Don't you want to return to your homeland?" asked Davian softly.

With all of the strength left in his body, Danilo nodded.

"You realize that you don't have to be here," Davian crooned. "You could be resting in a soft bed, or eating roast duck, or doing whatever you want. But instead you choose to be here, in this sad state. All because you refuse to provide me with a small bit of information."

Danilo said nothing. Even if he could think of anything to say, he had no energy left to voice it.

Frustrated, Davian grabbed Danilo's jaw roughly to force him to meet his gaze and squeezed his face firmly, causing the half-elf extreme pain as his own flesh pressed against his teeth and filled his mouth with the metallic taste of blood.

"I grow weary of your denial and your uselessness," Davian spat. "I want to know the way around the Tumultuous Bay!"

Danilo remained silent.

Davian threw back the man's head in anger after waiting for a few more moments. "You have until dusk to tell me how to get around the bay and into the secret cave. Although you feign ignorance, I know that you know the way. This is the last time I will ask you, worm. Are the dragons in the secret cave?"

With his eyes still closed, Danilo sent a weak message to his brother, but it was strong enough to let him know that he is still alive, though not for much longer.

Danelo stopped in a sort of jerky way and tilted his head downward as if saying a prayer. He raised his head and tilted it back, then uttered something in an Elvish language that the others obviously could not understand. In the quiet, his echoes could be heard throughout the empty marsh.

Hearing his brother's voice, Danilo's spirits lifted. Though he knew he was in pain, it was at least proof to him that he could be saved. "He's waiting fer us," he said and began hastily rushing through the wet bog that they'd reached.

Lorenz followed, though he did not like walking through the marshland. The deep mud sucked on his boots and made it hard to walk. If they got attacked here, it would be very difficult to fight. It made him nervous.

"It's best that we get through the marshland quickly," he said to everyone.

It appeared that the others were on the same page as Lorenz since they all picked up the pace, splashing the watery brown water all over themselves.

The oval red sun was now beginning to set, which only made Lorenz more apprehensive. He recited spell incantations in his head to keep them fresh, in case he would need to use them against anything creeping up on them.

Now midway into the marsh, Lorenz's fears were realized as the sun continued to lower and he heard soft distant splashing and saw ripples moving through the water.

"We must hurry," cautioned Danelo. "It isn't safe 'ere." His pace quickened even more. He was grunting with exertion, pulling his feet through the thick mud for so long.

Lorenz's gut agreed with him. They were in danger.

The party continued to navigate carefully and successfully through the marsh as the wind picked up, causing the tall reeds and spindly trees to dance in the breeze. All of a sudden, a shape rose out of the water with a sick slurping sound as it pulled up from the mud.

CHAPTER TWENTY-SEVEN: THE SEARCHES CONCLUSION

Dingle stopped from across the road and admired the large house before approaching it. It was huge and opulent— obviously very old and had a lot of effort and money put into its creation. The design sense of the builder, however, was another story. He smirked at the strange carvings and random shining colors of the house: purple, green, grey, gold, it was a color coordination mess. Then he began to walk towards the front steps.

Thiek, initially unaware that Dingle was about to enter his property, continued tending to the herbs his backyard. However, as soon as the sheriff placed his foot on the cobblestone path, the old man looked up alertly.

"Someone is walking up the path," he said aloud. "Oh, it's Dingle."

He stopped what he was doing and headed towards the house. As Dingle progressed up the walkway and neared the stairs, Thiek was coming through the living room and tidying up a bit in preparation for the visit.

Before Dingle could even reach the front door, Thiek opened the door and greeted him. "Welcome, Dingle."

"Hello, Thiek," he replied. "How are you today?"

"I'm doing well."

Thiek had lived in the house for many decades now. While he had never had personal brushes with the law, he had met Sheriff Dingle several times in the past on his travels into Nidum or other towns under his jurisdiction. Plus, as an old wise man, Dingle had occasionally come to ask him for advice on tough cases. The two had developed a mutual respect for each other over the years.

"What brings you to my humble abode?" Thiek asked.

"I heard that a foreign traveling stranger has been lurking near these parts after killing a few men. I was hoping to find him and question him about the slayings. Did he come this way? Have you seen him?" asked the sheriff.

Thiek clucked his tongue. "Hmmm, well... I heard something about a young man defending himself against some vicious robbers. From my understanding, they attacked him in his bed in the middle of the night. While defending himself, he unfortunately ended up mortally wounding them."

"You seem to know a lot about this man," Dingle commented.

"I suppose I do," Thiek answered playfully. "And you're looking to arrest him knowing this?"

"Please don't be dramatic, Thiek. I know Jbug's reputation," Dingle replied in exasperation. "But you must understand: this is my duty. If a crime occurs, no matter to whom, I must investigate it. I have an obligation to question the committer of any crime, whatever their reasons may have been, and I cannot turn a blind eye just because he's your friend."

Thiek held up his hands. "It is fine. If you just need to speak with him, that is your prerogative."

Dingle sighed in relief. "Thank you. I'm glad to finally have some headway in this investigation. Is he here right now?"

The old cigamian shook his head. "Sadly, he won't be back for a while. But I assure you that he is no murderer."

"I understand, Thiek. I am not here to carry him away in chains, you know. Can you please just tell me when will he return?"

The old man suddenly had a small sad look on his face that gave the sheriff an ominous feeling. Unbeknownst to the police officer, Thiek was turning over in his mind an entire world of worries. He wondered if Lorenz and the others were safe; he hoped that the captive man would be saved; he prayed that Lorenz found the dragons' cave before Davian did. Thiek smiled weakly and finally answered him.

"Not for a long while, Sheriff. You may want to head back to Nidum for a while before trying my door again. ...It is possible that he may not return at all."

CHAPTER TWENTY-EIGHT: INTO THE DARK

In seconds, Lorenzo's eyes cleared. He was outside on the sidewalk, surrounded by stores and restaurants. Judging from the street signs around him, he could tell that he was walking downtown towards K Street. This was on the way to school. It was a clear, chilly morning. It was a lot colder here in the real world, a far cry from the hot and humid swamp he'd just been in with the others.

On the upcoming corner, he noticed something that he was all too familiar with. Two teenage boys, probably upperclassmen, wearing letter jackets appeared to be harassing a smaller boy. It looked like they were attempting to take his wallet. No one would stop to help him, as everyone preferred to ignore the ugly events around them and keep their noses to their own business.

The bullies shoved the kid, pushed him and slapped him upside his head, jeering and cursing at him. His tear-stained face demonstrated his fear and anger. Lorenzo knew how he felt, all those times he'd been bullied and no one else stood up for him.

"I'm not going to let him go through what I went through. Even if no one else does anything, I'll be there for him." Lorenzo immediately started his trek across the street in the direction of the poor boy.

He was careful because it was a busy street with many cars and buses roaring by. After a few moments, there was a break in the traffic, which Lorenzo used to rush across. About ten feet away from them, he called out, "Hey! You guys should leave him alone."

The two older boys looked surprised as they looked at one another and then redirected their attentions to Lorenzo. "Yeah? What are you going to do?" asked the afro-headed taller boy dressed in a black jean jacket.

"I think you better go and mind your own business," barked the shorter skinny short-haired boy.

"He doesn't deserve to be treated like that," Lorenzo stressed.

"Why don't you take his place then," offered the afro-headed boy.

He stalked up to Lorenzo menacingly with a scowl. His body posture was aggressive and he meant to shove at Lorenzo. He was able to prepare for this by stepping away to the side just in the nick of time.

"You don't want to go down this road," Lorenzo suggested.

"What, you gonna call somebody for help?" he sneered and then again rushed towards Lorenzo.

He moved out of the way again in lightning speed, this time to the opposite direction, but now he noticed through his peripheral vision that the shorter bully getting closer. He meant to close in on Lorenzo to limit his movement, backing him into a corner. Noting this, Lorenzo sidestepped away from the other boy. While doing this, the taller one flew in for a punch. Without realizing his own movements, Lorenzo dodged to the left to avoid the blow, and then elbowed him sharply in the gut. The afro-headed boy hit the ground hard. The other boy stopped inching forward and went to help his friend up.

"This guy's a freak! I think we better leave this guy alone," said the afro-headed kid as he got back onto one knee, grimacing and holding his stomach.

"I think you're right," Lorenzo replied while looking daggers into his eyes.

The boys looked at him as if they'd seen a ghost. Just then, Lorenzo realized that he hadn't moved his lips when he'd replied to them, nor had the bully said those words out loud. He had read his mind and then responded telepathically, which terrified the boys. The shorter accomplice started to run away, leaving his friend kneeling on the ground. He got up in a panic and scrambled away as well. People cast sideways glances as they walked by.

"Are you okay?" he asked the younger kid, helping him up.

"Thank you," the boy said meekly, eyes downcast shyly.

"Sorry you had to go through that for me..."

Lorenzo pat him on the back reassuringly. "It's okay. This time. But people like me won't always be there to help you. In the future, you have to stand up for yourself. I know it's not easy, but don't let others walk all over you, okay?"

The boy nodded in embarrassment and his cheeks grew red.

"My name's Lorenzo, by the way," he offered and stuck out his hand cordially. "What's your name?"

The kid's wide hazel eyes grew misty and he took the hand. "My name is Jaime."

"Be not afraid. Trust your instincts. You will soon have an ally for life. He will help you when you meet the one you are destined to face."

Lorenz's whole body jerked. He was in the swamp water again, with putrid odors in his nostrils. An old man's voice had just filled his head and he was still working out what it had told him. Totally distracted by the voice, he didn't notice what was occurring in front of him.

"The monster!" he choked out.

The others were already way ahead of him, running as quickly as they could through the swamp. The water's height varied from ankle-deep to waist-deep in different areas as they fled. Lorenz hurried after them.

The mountain peaks seemed to hover above him in every direction, for how tall they were in the valley. "We have to climb over these? How will we ever get over them?" Lorenz asked himself.

Whatever had burst from the water and spooked everyone earlier was now out of sight again. The only evidence of the creature's existence—and pursuit—were all the unnatural ripples and swirls following in the water behind them. Following them.

In front of them was the mountain face with what seemed to be a small opening in the dirt, like a cave. They might be able to use the cave as shelter from whatever beast was chasing them.

"Guys! There's a cave over here!" Lorenz shouted, pointing to the dark opening. He headed in that direction, as did everyone else. Soon, they were out of the water and running on dry land again.

As if anticipating what they were trying to do, the monster burst forth from its hiding place in the muck. Lorenz wasn't looking back to see it, but he heard the enormous splash and shuffling as the beast hurtled after them. He then heard a loud hissing sound, but he didn't stop running. His waterlogged clothes and squishy boots weighed him down, but still they all ran.

About fifty feet from the entrance into the base of the mountain, Danelo stopped and spun around with his arrow in hand. The dwarves almost crashed into him.

"Lorenz, turn aroun'!" he shouted.

Lorenz quickly whirled in a 180 and pointed his sword in the direction of the noise. Okin and Unni also prepared their weapons with a level of fear on their faces. Danelo, knowing Lorenz was furthest back and the most in danger, speedily prepared his bow and arrow. His fingers moved so quickly that before Lorenz was even able to get a good eyeful of this menace, the arrow was on its way.

A screech pierced the quiet mountain air, emanating from a huge terrible maw. Lorenz's eyes took in the sight of the horrible beast stalking them, starting at the level of the water and rising up along its towering body to capture the full spectrum of this threat.

The beast was like some kind of crocodilian creature. Its eyes were beady yellow orbs with black pupil slits. The wide open screaming mouth was filled with many rows of crooked conical fangs, dripping with brown water and viscous saliva. It stood upright, almost like a gigantic man, except hunched over and covered in an armor of wet mud-caked scales.

Danelo quickly fired one more arrow, hitting the creature in its broad square shoulder. This stopped the raging beast only for a second as it realized what had just happened and then screeched shrilly to numb the pain. Its eyes blazed as it reared up and barreled towards its assailant and his friends. The monster's slimy skin glistened in the evening light and it stank of the rancid marsh waters. Mud flung in every which direction as the lizard-like water beast charged.

Lorenz and the others quickly entered the small tunnel in the side of the mountain with Danelo running to catch up and following behind. The moment they all entered the rocky passage, it was impossible to see as the twisting narrow passage allowed no outside light to penetrate the darkness.

Unable to see, Lorenz couldn't tell how Danelo sealed the opening to the entrance, but with a gravelly grinding sound, it closed off before the snarling creature could reach them. Animal screams of anger were heard muffled from outside through the stony blockade.

Everyone stopped to catch their breath. Lorenz exhaled in relief and the dwarves wiped warm sweat from their bushy brows. He took the time to wring out the hem of his tunic and his sleeves and dumped out the excess water in his boots. The dwarves and Danelo followed in suit. Lorenz's clothes were still soaking wet, but he was just glad to be safe from the huge reptilian beast. After he was able to calm down long enough and the adrenaline has mostly cleared from his system, Lorenz squinted into the gloom to try to take a look around. It would be impossible to see at all if it weren't for a few slivers of daylight seeping in from a few gaps and cracks in the rock walls and ceiling.

"Stay close t'gether or else," Danelo advised calmly in the darkness.

Lorenz nodded and followed after the tall man's silhouette, listening to the echoes of their footsteps on the dusty stone floor as they inched forward. He felt one of the dwarves bumped into him from behind, though he couldn't tell if it was Okin or Unni.

"Ouch! Watch where ya goin'," one of the brothers grumbled irritably under his breath as the two apparently collided again in the blackness with a telltale clanking of metal.

"We need light," Lorenz thought to himself with a sigh. Without any indication, the gem inside his pocket lit up, shining clearly through the fabric. He jumped in surprise, then took the gem out and held it high in the air to light their way.

Lorenz instinctively shielded his eyes with his free hand, but quickly realized that even though the artifact he held glowed extremely brightly to illuminate the cavern, the light somehow did not burn his fingers nor did it hurt his eyes. With the help of the gem, everyone could now appreciate the surroundings that they were in. The passage they were in had led to a huge cave. Directly in front of the group was a major drop off. As they surveyed the expansive cavern, Lorenz saw a trail that circled around the roughly round chamber, spiraling downwards.

The cavern must have been over 500 feet in diameter and the huge hollow chamber ran even deeper. In spite of the luminosity of the gem in his hand, Lorenz still couldn't make out the bottom floor below them. The path went incredibly deep underground. The seemingly bottomless climb took Lorenz's breath away.

Though the stone walls and floors around them looked naturalistic, it was clear that the path they were walking on had been formed and maintained at some point in the past by human hands. The walls were rugged with roughly hewn ridges and jagged edges. The earth could be seen in distinct strata in the rocky surfaces, too many of various compositions and colors for Lorenz to differentiate for sure. He could recall from his high school science class a few of the layers, noting the shining veins of crystalline white quartz, the dark reds of oxidized ferrous soils, and the black strips of slate and coal.

The colorful portraiture trailing through the earth was lovely on its own, but still another beautiful spectacle also greeted their eyes. Just a couple hundred feet below them were amazing carvings, wrought right from the stone itself, creating statues and frescoes and even buildings. It was like an ancient civilization had painstakingly carved and built an entire city into the underground cliff face and then had long since vanished, leaving the place dark and lonely to gather dust.

Okin whistled at the sight. "Pretty view here, ya think so?"

Danelo grunted in response. "Perhaps the beauty is lost on me fer the moment. Let's keep goin'," he replied impatiently and hurried down the trail.

Pebbles and small rocks ticked against the ground and rolled off the steep walkway as they all descended.

"Careful guys," Lorenz warned. A simple stumble could spell an unlucky man certain doom in this place.

"Ya, we will," replied Unni. "Tha' gem ya have is a great help," he added appreciatively.

"Yeah," smiled Lorenz.

The four men continued to rush down the gradually spiraling path, passing by countless engraved marble figures and granite pillars. It reminded Lorenz a little bit of ancient Greek art and architecture, splashed with other cultural flairs. He didn't get to enjoy the scene for long before the half-elf before them stopped short in his tracks.

Lorenz almost crashed into him before he could stop his momentum on the sloped pathway. "What is it?"

"We are not alone," Danelo said suddenly. "Something terrible is 'ere. Something that could be our demise."

Lorenz wouldn't have been too alarmed about the warning if it weren't for the expression on the Elvisan's face. Normally cool and stoic, Danelo's features now read only fear. The hair creeped up on Lorenz's neck as his heart raced in the silence and his legs began to quiver uncontrollably.

Lorenz glanced down at his feet in surprise at his trembling. Within seconds, the shaking had stopped and a low rumbling emerged from the darkness below them, making him realize that it hadn't been his legs shaking, but rather the entire cave had been distantly vibrating.

He had no idea what had caused the frightening quake,

but he didn't like the idea of having to go closer to the source. Lorenz's mind raced with possibilities. A voice within him spoke to him, saying: "It is all right. This force with aid you greatly. You must have trust."

Lorenz glanced around at his friends, but it seemed that only he had heard the cryptic advice. Supposedly, he had to trust whatever had made that terrifying noise.

Unni and Okin exchanged worried looks and they whispered something to one another in dwarvish.

Danelo was the first to speak aloud after the groaning from the earth had finally ceased. Lorenz grasped the gem in his hand tighter as the emerald-eyed man spoke.

"Gather yer courage, comrades. We must continue, even in the face of danger—or death."

CHAPTER TWENTY-NINE: TAKING HOSTAGE

With a heavy heart, Sheriff Dingle had no choice but to return to his hometown of Nidum. The old man Thiek had told him that the suspect named Lorenz would not be returning for a long while, and he knew that Thiek was a man of his word. Continuing to search for him now was pointless.

The front door jingled as the sheriff walked into the office.

"Sheriff!" cried the deputy, jumping from where he'd been lounging back in his seat with his feet up on the desk. "You're back!"

Dingle shrugged. "I've only been gone for a few days, Rangle. No need to get excited."

"It's been over a week, Sheriff!" he exclaimed again. "I was beginning to wonder if you'd wandered into someplace you shouldn't've."

Dingle smiled. "Well, now you know I'm fine. I was never in any danger. Investigating is my life."

The deputy sank back into his chair, but he kept his feet on the ground this time. He looked at Dingle and replied, "I just dunno sometimes, Sheriff. The world's getting to be a dangerous place out there. And then you have this knack of ruffling some feathers sometime, you know?"

Sheriff Dingle ignored him. "Could you just give me an update on how things have been while I've been gone?"

Rangle quickly wrangled up some files from a drawer in his work desk. "Here's everything. Not much. A few minor offenses. A pickpocketing... some instances of vandalism... a civil disturbance between the baker and candlestick maker... I've got it all under control. And... Oh." The deputy stopped short.

"Oh?" Dingle echoed.

"Well, there is something you may wanna check out now that you're back, Sheriff. Though I may not think it's the brightest idea..."

"I'll be the judge of that, Deputy."

"Yes, of course, Sheriff," Rangle nodded. "Well, you know old Jbug's house?"

Dingle's eyes shone and his brows rose at the mention of the victim's name. He'd just given up on the case for the time being, but now someone else had brought it up to him. "What about the house?"

Rangle rubbed the back of his neck sheepishly. "Well... Me and the boys, we tried our best to keep the crime scene under wraps for you for when you got back. You know we did-"

"What happened, Rangle?" he demanded. "Spit it out."

"There was a... disturbance there. A group of about six ruffians decided to move in there just a couple days ago. We tried to explain to them that it was a crime scene under investigation and that they had to leave, but they weren't very... cooperative."

"So, you just let them be?" Dingle asked incredulously.

"I'm sorry, Sheriff," he sighed in response. "They weren't bothering nobody there, it seemed. And they were getting mighty rowdy when we tried to get them to leave. They seem to know Jbug. I think they're his friends or relatives, Sheriff. They wouldn't tell us why they were in the house though. They just said they wanted to speak to the sheriff."

"That's just great," Dingle groaned. "Fine. I'll go and deal with them."

Rangle burst from his seat again. "What!? Sheriff, no! That folk is dangerous! They ain't your average shoemaker, if that's what you're thinking!"

"Stand down, Deputy. I can handle it."

"But it must be a trap, sir!" Rangle added. "At least wait for daylight tomorrow before you go-"

He didn't let Rangle argue with him any further. Without so much as even getting a moment to sit down and rest at his office after all his traveling, Sheriff Dingle was out the door and on the case again. He had to see what his group of trespassers wanted.

The sun had already been setting when Dingle had

gotten back to Nidum. Now the moon was beginning to rise and shine. Town workers were beginning to light a few street lamps in the busier areas of town, but most of the streets were still dark at night. Even in the darkness, Dingle could easily remember the way to the old house.

It wasn't longer before he arrived at the crime scene where he'd vowed to find the killer. And now he'd come back empty-handed. He clomped up the splintery wooden steps, took a deep breath, and knocked on the front door solidly three times.

Moments later, he heard a shuffling from indoors and a gravelly voice from inside asked what he wanted.

"I'm the sheriff. I heard you wanted to speak to me."

A moment's silence passed before the door clicked open. Dingle's heart skipped a beat as he saw the rabble that awaited him on the other side. He began to regret not taking Rangle's advice of waiting until the next day.

Lit up by the yellow light of several small hand lanterns were the sour faces of six grungy men outfitted in dirty leather travel clothes. Sharp blades hung at their sides, also shining gold in the lamplight.

"Glad to see you could finally make it, Sheriff," said one man in the forefront. He must've been the leader of the group. Underneath the dirt and soiled clothes, he was a good-looking man in his thirties, lean but well-muscled.

He drew closer the Dingle, close enough for him to smell the odor of old sweat coming off from his clothes. "Now that you're here, we can actually get started." His face was a mixture of twisted amusement and smoldering hostility. "Take me to where my nephew is buried."

The five men behind the leader hurried forward, shoving Dingle off the porch and down the steps with them.

"They're in the local town cemetery," Dingle replied between shoves. He worked his way to the front of the gang, leading them with quick strides to the graveyard on the outskirts of town, not too far from Jbug's house.

"Buried like stray dogs amongst your toothless bums,"

spat a squatter man with a long scar on his face.

"No," Dingle retorted. "Buried with dignity, as all men should be."

"High words for a sheriff who's been skirting his civic duty all week," the leader continued. "Did you enjoy your little vacation?"

"I have spent this past week to search for the perpetrator of this heinous crime, in fact," Dingle replied coolly.

The leader looked slightly amused. "Then, you'll have to introduce me to the one who did this. Surely you've caught him after all this time."

Dingle's face flushed with shame.

"Your silence speaks for itself, Sheriff."

He tried to avert the topic for a moment. "Speaking of introductions, you gentlemen know who I am, but how am I to address each of you?"

The men exchanged curious glances and the leader nodded with a smile. A tall, slim fellow with dark brown messy hair spoke first.

"My name is Rogg." He then pointed to another tall man, except this one was blond with a big pointed nose. "That one's Gree."

"I'm Jar," added a short, stocky man with thick burly arms. He had walnut-colored eyes and hair, surprisingly fair compared to the rest of his otherwise unattractive body. "The others are Raij and JJ."

Another squat but robust man, with the scarred face and black hair nodded at the name Raij. An averagely-built wiry young man with curly locks glowered at Dingle upon the mention of the name JJ.

"And you can call me Rijo," spoke the leader at last.

"Thank you kindly," the sheriff said, trying to sound amenable despite the situation. "As you already know, I'm Sheriff Dingle."

They had reached the small cemetery by now. It was both peaceful and eerie at night. Not a place that Dingle visited often.

"Your nephew and his friends should be buried in the new ground over here," Dingle stated, leading them to the open land at the edge, where more plots were being readied.

Angry growls were heard when the six men arrived at Jbug's and the others' graves. Dingle immediately saw what had made them so upset. The fresh gravestones had been knocked over and obscene graffiti was scrawled upon the stones. No doubt, bitter townsfolk who'd lost something precious to the hoodlums had come to vandalize the graves.

"I'll file a report and get this cleaned up," the sheriff said quickly to try to appease them.

"Never mind," Rijo replied. Despite the weight of the rock, the man easily lifted the headstone from the soil with one hand and pushed it back into place.

"Enough of this farce! Where is the man who killed them?" Gree hissed angrily to the sheriff as his narrow eyes gleamed with grief and hate. The simple stone graves he stood over shone somberly under the moonlight.

"We're still searching for him," Dingle replied in a tight voice.

"Well, maybe you aren't looking hard enough," retorted Rijo. "They've been dead for weeks, Sheriff, and you have nothing to show for it. I'm thinking that perhaps you aren't properly motivated..."

Sweat soaked Sheriff Dingle's collar and the pits of his shirt. The six men before him were furious; they might snap at any moment or at the wrong words, so he chose his response carefully. "I assure you, I am trying my hardest and I will not rest until the killer is found."

The rugged-looking men quietly glanced amongst one another, weighing his statement silently. Finally, their leader Rijo nodded subtly and spoke.

"Fine. But from here on, we will help you look," he said through gritted teeth.

"Really, sirs, I have it under control," suggested Dingle gently.

"Yeah, I can see that from all the progress you've made

on the investigation," drawled JJ sarcastically, showing yellowed crooked teeth in a nasty sneer. "Our hard-earned tax dollars are going to great use," he snickered.

Dingle held his tongue.

"We will not tolerate any more of your incompetence in this search. You will accept my men's' help..." Rijo waved his hand towards the center of Nidum. "Or the people of your town will pay the price for this filthy murderer."

Raij, the short and stocky brute with the ugly scar, raised his sword to the level of Dingle's throat. "I would agree to the generous offer if'n I were you, Sheriff."

Giving in to the threats of criminals and extortionists was not something that Dingle was used to doing, but there was no other choice. Seeing their stony faces illuminated to look even colder than tombstones in the moonlight, he knew these men meant business. They wouldn't hesitate to harm innocent people in their quest for vengeance.

There was not a large enough police force in the town to be able to fend off a surprise attack from these hardened men, at least not without heavy casualties. If it saved peoples' lives, Dingle would travel alongside the group of thugs as their personal private investigator and hostage.

"Fine, we will travel together to search for him," Dingle acquiesced. "But please let me advise my deputy before I must go again."

Rijo nodded. "You have until noon to return to meet with us again in front of the house tomorrow."

Dingle nodded back. The deal was set.

CHAPTER THIRTY: FOREBODING

"Get up," growled a commanding voice.

A sharp pain in the ribs told Danilo that he'd just been kicked from where he lay curled up on the floor in chains. His breath caught in his throat and though he wanted to comply to avoid further punishment, he was too weak to move. Danilo's "caretaker," growing weary of waiting, decided to help the battered fellow up.

"Get up!" He yanked him by the right arm. Hard. The muscles and tendons stretched to their fullest limit, sending desperate signals of pain throughout his entire body.

"Agh!" Danilo cried. "Please..." He fought back tears and struggled to his knees, then using his cuffed hands as a brace against the wall, tried to get onto his wobbly feet. The soft clinking of metal and a sudden resistance demonstrated to Danilo that the chains around his arms and neck had reached their bounds.

Seeing this, the grubby caretaker retrieves a rusted key from his pocket and unlocks the steel neck brace. "Hurry up now. Master Davian doesn't have all day, you scum," he barked.

Though it was bright in the room due to the bright light streaming in through the open door, Danilo could hardly make out anyone's faces due to how swollen his face had become, obscuring his vision. He kept one eye closed, preferring the half-vision to the horrible ache he felt while keeping them both open. He tried to glance around his environment as he stepped forward in the cramped wooden chambers, hoping for the tiniest change of escape.

He took each step slowly, deliberately, and cautiously. He felt the weight of his heavy body on his grimy toes, the splintery wood plank floors. He felt the cool brush of the wind blowing in from outside, felt the forgotten warmth of the daylight sun on his skin. Finally, breaking forth from the doorway from his hellhole, he was outside once again. He had long lost count of how many days he'd been trapped inside his torture chamber. He tried to take a deep breath of the salty fresh air and his one good eye wandered to the edge of the ship, where he saw the rolling ocean waves beckoning to him. He wondered what chances he would have of escaping his cruel captors if he made a dash for the railing now-

SMACK!

Another muscular henchman backhanded Danilo again, sending bright little stars into his field of vision. He gasped and hung limply in his chains.

"This is your last chance, vermin. Where is the location? I won't ask again."

It might have been Davian speaking this time. Danilo couldn't even tell who was saying what anymore. Everyone's faces and voices were becoming a blur. He just kept picturing the beautiful blue freedom of the sea. How he wished he could just swim away.

"Fine. Your choice-"

"...It's north..." he croaked. "North o' th'bay..."

Danilo couldn't even recognize his own voice. The words had been so weak and scratchy, and blood flew out in red flecks as he spoke. He breathed heavily after saying only those few words and waited.

A few moments later, a hand patted his bruised and beaten shoulder softly. "Now see, that wasn't so hard, was it?" Davian crooned gently. "Cooperation deserves reward."

The darkly-clad cigamian signaled to his men. "Feed him a good dinner tonight; help him get his strength back," he ordered. "He needs to be fit to travel by tomorrow."

Danilo heard a shuffling of footsteps leaving the room, presumably to bring his some food and water. He didn't know if he could even muster the energy to sit up and drink through his split lips.

"You're lucky, you know?" Davian continued in his half-sweet, half-menacing tone. "It's roast beef tonight. You'll enjoy it, I'm sure. After how long it's been since you've eaten, you skinny thing."

The Elvisan stayed slumped silently, trying to focus his tired mind on sending a telepathic message to his brother. It was short and simple. "Find me, brother. By tomorrow, you will not see me alive."

The cigamian suddenly grasped Danilo's discolored face, causing him to yelp in pain.

"Maybe you need a little help here."

Davian took out his wand, which emitted a blue-green flash of light over Danilo's bruised and broken skin. Gradually, the dull aches in his muscles and sharp pains in his skin lessened and wounds slowed and stopped their bleeding. His clothes and skin were still filthy from weeks of being unable to wash, but at least the injuries were healing up.

Danilo looked up into Davian's fiery eyes as the strength seeped back into his weary bones.

"Help me and you receive more of that," Davian smiled disingenuously and gestured towards the open sea. "However, if you try to or if you lie to me, I will make sure that you suffer a slow and painful death."

Danilo grimaced and hung his head again, this time in resignation rather than weakness. He did not bother to gaze upon the ocean again. He had no chance to get away with Davian watching.

Davian put his wand away and turned around to leave the room. "I will get my dragon."

A few sailors escorted Danilo away to get washed up and fed, leaving Davian alone on the deck. The wind whipped his silver-streaked hair and robes, invigorating him. A wry smile broadened across his face, lingering there for many minutes until a sense of foreboding washed over him.

"Wait. What's this I feel?" he asked himself. "Someone out there intends to challenge me." Davian's eyes seemed to spark as he stood defiantly. "But he will never defeat me. The dragons are mine."

CHAPTER THIRTY-ONE: CHOICES

They were traveling down the tall dark spiraling trail. Traveling to the source of the rumbling noise. Lorenz felt dizzy. At first, he thought it was just because of the fear or the vertigo, but it was soon evident that this was not the case.

He was back to the place where it had all began: the little alley outside his Aunt Georgia's home. Lorenzo looked around. The place seemed largely unchanged from how he had last seen it, but there were subtle differences. The patch of weeds that the gem had been hidden under was gone; the litter on the ground had been cleaned up. The chain link fence had been replaced by a nice new wooden fence.

Lorenzo stepped out of the narrow alley and back onto the street. Aunt Georgia's house had been repainted a reddish brown terracotta color. He then remembered that she no longer lived here; the new owners must have redone the home.

Her house wasn't the only one that was different. The whole neighborhood had been changing. The seedy corner store had been spruced up. Where there had once been a shady little establishment with cracked tinted windows covered in faded ads was now a fresh convenience store. The windows were clean and large and the outdoor façade was inviting. He headed over to the store to check out the place.

There were a few young adults hanging outside the doors just chatting. It was no one Lorenzo could recognize. They were probably new to the area, or maybe they lived in a different neighborhood nearby. He didn't stop to ask.

Lorenzo went inside and enjoyed the cool blast of the AC air on his hot skin, a welcome change from the muggy heat outside. Feeling a little thirsty, he walked over to the cold beverages aisle and began browsing around the fridges with the sodas. While he looked around, he overheard some people talking from the next aisle over. He would have eavesdropped except that they were talking about some happenings in the area.

Some kids he knew from one of the schools he'd gone to has recently been killed. It was Jay and Willie. Lorenzo's heart skipped a beat nervously when he heard the news. They'd been killed over some drug-related money issues just last year, apparently in some big fiasco that had been all over the news.

"How sad," Lorenzo thought to himself. They had been jerks in school, but didn't deserve that. "What choices did they make in their lives that led them down that path?"

He felt terrible for their families, but evidently, it had been their deaths that had helped spark a huge renovation in the area. People started to clean up. The changes in the beginning were small and subtle. Jay's brothers quit selling drugs and started working legitimate jobs and began volunteering in anti-drug campaigns to reach out to other troubled youths. Trying to move on from the tragedy, Willie's family spent their time grieving to remodel their entire house, causing a chain reaction down the block and beyond of other families deciding to fix up their homes too. Roofs were re-shingled, garages outfitted with fancy new doors with fancy window designs, paint jobs redone, and flowers and colorful shrubs and rock gardens replaced the yellowed weedy lawns that once graced the streets. The air of change gradually spread and created a great new atmosphere for the neighborhood, filled with more hope and goodwill than ever before.

Lorenzo grabbed a chilled Pepsi from the refrigerator and headed towards the checkout counter, glancing back quickly to see who had been talking in the snack aisle next to him. However, he didn't recognize these people either.

He paid for the soda with some of the cash in his pocket and stepped back out into the heat. It seemed strangely peaceful being back here in the neighborhood that he had once hated so much. He almost wanted to go back into the crisply cooled convenience store, avoiding the summer heat and just chill there, gossiping with the others. But Lorenzo remained outside, shielding his eyes from the midday sun and watching over the houses and stores and streets, his old neighborhood, and felt a twinge of pride at how much it had improved over the years he'd been gone.

He walked down the sidewalk, to sure where he was heading to, but it didn't bother him. He had choices. It wasn't like when he was a little kid and felt like he had no control over anything. Now, he could go anywhere he wanted and do anything. He could walk down to the arcade or library, or take a bus to the bowling alley or park. This free summer day was his to seize. However, the choice was made for him.

Lorenzo dug into his pocket with disappointment as the gem began to vibrate again. He actually wanted to stay. With a sigh, he let himself be taken back to the mountain cave.

CHAPTER THIRTY-TWO: KNIFE TO THE THROAT

Sheriff Dingle sprinted back to his office in record time. Panting as he walked up the stairs, on the verge of passing out, he reached the front door and knocked weakly.

The deputy opened up for him and led Dingle inside. "Uh, hey, Boss. You getting some exercise?"

"No," Dingle gasped. "I have to go again."

Rangle looked perplexed. "Go? You just got back here!" he exclaimed.

Dingle rushed to his desk and grabbed his tote bag. He rummaged through the drawers, filling it up with all the necessities he could think of. "I have to lead a search party. They'll help me find him."

"Don't tell me-"

"Yes," Dingle cut him off. "We're looking for the killer."

Deputy Rangle sighed in surrender. "Fine, Boss. You're the sheriff. I can't argue with you. You're too stubborn for that."

Dingle began silently going through the cabinets on the back wall of the office.

"Excited, Sheriff?"

"No, Rangle. But I have to do this. Please trust me." Dingle closed up his bag and splashed some water from a pitcher onto his sweaty face.

"Do you need any help?" Rangle asked.

"Yes, Deputy. Your job is terribly important," the sheriff said gravely. "Please make sure that Nidum is safe while I am gone. Take care of the town."

The deputy's eyes narrowed in concern. "Yes, of course, Boss."

Dingle nodded curtly and waved goodbye, then rushed out of the office in a blur. Rangle saw him run down the street, back to the direction of Jbug's old house.

Shaking his head, Rangle shut the front door and fell back down upon his seat. "Man, I've never seen Boss act like that before. The way he was moving, you'd think someone were holding a knife to his throat."

CHAPTER THIRTY-THREE: DRAGON HEART

Lorenz had been called back. They were in the dim caves again, but now the trail branched to another tubular cavern. He knew they had to go this way. "Be not afraid," the voice in his head told him.

He held the gem forward to light the way in the dank tunnel. However, the smell of the moist cool cavern seemed to suddenly change at this point. It was incredibly warmer in this cave and it almost smelled like... burning. A breeze sucked in and out gently, as if the tunnel were breathing.

His hairs felt like they were standing straight up. "I can do this. I know it," he whispered to himself.

Danelo, Okin and Unni were all bravely soldiering on. With his friends by his side, he knew he could conquer anything.

"Can it-ah be?" gasped Unni. He was beginning to think the same thing that Lorenz and everyone else was thinking.

Lorenz's memories flickered back to the soul room, his bedroom in Thiek's mansion. The paintings across the walls were covered with dragons. Could it be a dragon that was waiting for him at the end of this tunnel?

The group pressed on slowly and cautiously, with Lorenz at the forefront, holding his light aloft. Little by little, he could make out more of the resting creature's gargantuan body. First, he saw the tip of a huge ridged horn which seemed to go on forever in the shadows. As he drew closer, he saw that it was attached to a huge scaly red mass.

Noticing the visitors, the creature raised itself up from where it lay and it stepped forward into the light to peer at Lorenz. It was magnificent. The scales were huge and glossy, like smooth red-hot pebbles. The musculature was well defined for a creature living so deep underground. The intense eyes gazing down upon him were big and intelligent.

Lorenz's initial fear began to dissipate. He could tell that this being meant him no harm. He remembered what Thiek had told him the first day they had met. "You have the heard of a dragon."

He felt Danelo and the dwarves watching him quietly from the side as the dragon sized him up.

"I'm here to aid you," a voice spoke to Lorenz in a language he didn't know, but could understand. "All you need to do is call my name: Silver."

With that message, the dragon, Silver, disappeared. Gone. Lorenz was floored. He didn't know what to do. The others stood still, not moving a muscle, as if they too had seen a ghost.

"Hey guys, that was pretty cool, huh?" Lorenz asked the dwarf brothers, but they remained in stunned silence.

"C'mon," Danelo finally said. "We must go."

The four men hurried back onto the trail and up the other branch. It was going up and up. Lorenz wondered if they were going to come out of the mountainside soon. He wanted to see Silver some more, but he knew they had no time to waste.

They kept climbing in an uncomfortable silence. Lorenz figured at least Okin would have made some kind of joke or whine about his tired wet feet by now, but everyone was strangely quiet.

"How in th'name o' LoLoric did yeh get a dragon?" Danelo muttered as they climbed.

They must have ascended at least several hundred feet before arriving at a dead end. Rather, it was an exit, but it was closed shut. The door was circular and set flush in the smooth rocky mountain wall. The outline was clear though and they could see light shining through the edges from the other side.

Danelo examined the ancient-looking door and pressed the circular door. Lorenz noted that he used his right hand to touch the exit in a clockwise circle. First, the top, then right side, then bottom, and finally the left. When he'd finished, the door rose up into the wall with a low grind, revealing a hallway with smoothed carved walls that led to the outside.

They wasted no time in reveling in their freedom. They hurried down the mountain trail under the light of the red sunset. Trees dotted the scrubby landscape in a sort of chaparral-like setting, their leaves aglow with the ember light. The trail became less distinct and the trees more numerous and scraggly, twisting this way and that as they continued, confusing Lorenz as to which way they should go. He was glad that Danelo was leading the way because it was easy to get lost in this mess. The twisted trees had become a maze.

Danelo was the first to address Lorenz. "So, yeh've been keepin' something from us, eh?" he said aloud with clear irritation.

Lorenz was taken aback, shaking his hands. "No way! I wasn't keeping anything from you guys!"

"Well, I mus' say, I was a bit surprised when th'dragon jus' decided t'come to yeh!" Danelo retorted.

"It-ah was a surprise ta us, too," Unni admitted.

So that was why everyone had been so quiet. They had begun to doubt him. Lorenz felt a little angry at their mistrust. "I didn't know about any of this!" he cried. "Why would I hide this from you?

"Well, at-ah least we don't have ta worry about-ah Davian getting' this one!" Okin said optimistically.

"Never mind," Danelo sighed. "There isn't time t'argue about this."

"Ya, it's nearly dark. It's time ta set camp soon," Okin agreed.

"No," Danelo replied shortly. "No time t'camp either. We keep moving. We can rest a few hours at best."

Okin groaned. "Tha's gonna be hard-ah going, though," he began to argue.

"Meh brother is dying," Danelo growled. "I won't let it be because of yer laze, dwarf."

Okin's cheeks grew red. "Ya callin' me lazy, elf?"

Lorenz's head jerked in place as he heard a message from Thiek. "Davian is on his way to your location. You need to move! Head on the trail to the east." He shook his head and took Okin by the shoulder. "Stop, Okin. Danelo is right. We can't stop. It's too dangerous now. Davian is coming.

Thiek just told me."

"Davian?" Danelo hissed. "He'll have meh brother with him, leadin' th'way."

"Probably. You think we can take him?" Lorenz asked nervously.

"Bring 'em on!" cried Okin. "It's what-ah we've all been-ah wanting." His brother clapped Okin's back in stout agreement.

Lorenz felt a little heartened by his friends' passion. Maybe they could do it after all; maybe they could stop the world's most powerful cigamian.

Even Danelo seemed encouraged by the brighter spirits. "Well, we don't have time to camp th'whole night, but we can rest a few hours at th'least."

The men all agreed that it was a good idea and decided to partially set up a resting ground a ways down the trail by a stand of trees. It was already fairly late and the last light had faded away.

Under their quickly set up tent, the dwarves were already snoring away when Lorenz laid his head down upon his own blanket under the stars. They planned to get up in just a couple hours to continue on the way. With the songs of owls and crickets to lull him to slumber, Lorenz would have been able to fall asleep quickly as well if it weren't for the disturbing noises he heard that were growing gradually louder. They were voices—human voices in the distance.

Danelo heard them too. He flipped open the dwarves' tent and tapped each of them on the side to wake them up. "People are getting close. Bad people. We gotta go now," he urged.

"Do you think it's Davian and his gang?" Lorenz asked.

"Mos' likely," the half-elf agreed with glimmering eyes.

Lorenz read the expression on Danelo's face and felt bad for him. The man must be so torn, knowing that he was so close to rescuing his long lost brother, but still having to run from his captors.

"Le's jes keep going. We're not safe," he added grimly.

"Ya," Unni concurred. "But-ah do you hear tha other sound-ah too?"

Danelo's pointed ears perked up. "Yes, more trouble."

Lorenz strained to hear it too. It seemed to be a skittering sound, then sort of a clicking. "It's getting closer to us, and fast!"

Danelo pointed his traveling torch towards the bushes several yards before them. Lorenz pulled out his gem to help light the way. At first, they could only make out some shadows in the darkness scurrying along the ground. Then four small crawling creatures emerged from the brush, seemingly sniffing out the men. They looked a little bit like very large black beetles with shiny accordion-ridged carapaces. Several pairs of hairy antennae waves hungrily in the air, smelling for food.

"That's it?" Lorenz laughed. "I almost got worried for a second." His tensed sword arm relaxed at his side. They couldn't have been any larger than squirrels. The small animals seemed easy to scare away or dispatch.

"Don't-ah be fooled," warned Okin. "We've-ah seen these-ah before. This species can-ah grow many times-ah their size."

Danelo must have agreed because he was already reaching back for an arrow.

Lorenz soon saw that the dwarf was right. The beetles he'd seen just a second ago the size of rodents were already the size of a house cat. They had inflated their bodies, puffing out the accordion sides to grow tremendously fast. Lorenz reached for his sword once more. Within a few more blinks, they were already the size of Labradors. How much bigger were they going to get?

Danelo's first arrow whizzed by, striking one of the beetles in the side of the thorax. A sharp crack pierced the air, but the arrow seemed to glance off the tough exoskeleton after cracking it. The animal took a few steps back with its spindly legs, chattering its pointy mandibles and releasing a hissing noise. Knowing the fight was far from over, Danelo was already readying another arrow.

He wouldn't be able to shoot them fast enough though, especially considering how hard their shells were. Unni had joined in by now, also firing with his own bow and arrow, hitting another beetle in the head, breaking off an antenna.

The beetles were swift in retaliation. Their long legs carried them frighteningly rapidly, like giant roaches. Surrounding the two archers, Okin lunged in with his axe to defend the men who were busy reloading. He crashed the heavy axe blade down satisfyingly on the abdomen of the beetle with the missing antenna, crunching the glossy outer elytra. The animal screeched with a tinny buzzy quality and staggered. Though he'd gotten a good hit in, Okin had put himself into grave danger as he'd made himself the main target for the four beasts. And though they now the size of goats, they were still growing!

Lorenz knew he had to end the battle quickly lest one of them get severely injured in the fight. He thought back to his lessons with Thiek and knew what to do. He set aside his blade and envisioned a hot white bolt of lightning striking the monsters then he pulled out his wand.

It was too dark at night to see the dark clouds forming, but within seconds, the lightning appeared and shot forward into one beetle, cleaving the gnashing head into two. It fell dead before Okin, twitching a little bit and sizzling.

"Whoa!" cried the dwarf.

There were still three more however and they seemed unfazed by the spell that had taken down one of their brethren.

"Unni! Danelo! Move!" Lorenz cried.

The bow-slingers didn't need to be told twice. They dodged out of the way as the beetles chased after them. Lorenz pointed his wand again and aimed carefully with both his hand and his mind, focusing intently on only hitting the pursuing multi-legged monster.

This time, the lightning bolt struck dead in the center of the beetle, making the entire gut contents of the overgrown arthropod explode in a loud boom. Hot bits of funky-smelling goo and shards of carapace littered the ground around them. Its lifeless body collapsed on the earth like a sack of lead.

As this was happening, one of the remaining insects dove forward and managed to graze Danelo's midsection with its knife-like jaws, making him grunt in pain. Lorenz's mind raced. The animal was too close for him to dare use another lightning spell, as it might hit Danelo too. Thinking quickly, Lorenz pictured the creature lifting up into the air, just as he had practiced with some of Thiek's household objects so long ago.

Before it was able to lunge again for the kill, the beetle floated up into the air, and it thrashed its legs around frantically in confusion. "Clear out of the way!" Lorenz warned. He brought the creature up to the level of the tall tree canopy and then let it fall to the ground with a dull crunch. The spatter of insect blood sprayed them all as the body walls burst open on impact.

The immediate threat was now over as the only beetle left was the one Okin had injured, which he and Unni finished off with ease. Lorenz breathed a sigh of relief.

"Good job," said Danelo.

"Thanks." Lorenz smiled and put away his wand, but as he did, his whole body felt a strange twinge which he'd never experienced before.

"What is it?" he asked.

"I don't know," Lorenz replied. "I think it's a sense. I think it means that someone else with powerful cigam is near. Someone dangerous."

Danelo nodded. "Yeh, it's Davian fer certain. We must devise a plan."

CHAPTER THIRTY-FOUR: LOST IN THE NIGHT

With Danilo leading the ground team that Davian had organized, the cigamian and his men shuffled off the ship and onto land. Danilo called out to his brother to hurry, as it would not be long before Davian would find the dragons' mountain, and before he would inevitably be killed.

They had the half-elf in chains like before, to make sure that he wouldn't run away while leading them. They'd outfitted him in a clean pair of trousers and a sailor's tunic like the others after he'd washed himself up. Danilo was kept in a lead wagon with several guards, just to be safe. Davian was a cautious man and wouldn't have his most valuable person in danger of getting lost.

"This way," Danilo said sullenly. He led the caravan through an overgrown trail towards the mountains. Clearly, no one had been this way in many years, and the trail has become quite bumpy and rough. Men had to be stationed in front of the wagons with machetes in order to clear the vines and shrubs out of the way for the wagons' wheels. Thanks to the dense vegetation, their traveling speed was severely reduced and the daylight hours and the men's strength quickly waned.

With night rapidly falling, Davian knew that he would soon have to call for camp. "Useless, weak men," he thought to himself, as he had the energy to walk a hundred mountains before having to stop for rest.

"Men! We camp in this site," he commanded. "We continue at daybreak!"

Davian dismounted from his personal carriage and headed into the tent that some of his henchman had speedily prepared for him. The sounds of men shouting orders and clearing brush continued for hours into the night as the entire group cleared enough space to set up their tents and settle down.

Suddenly a commotion began to brew late into the night. Davian opened the flap to his tent and stepped out, checking on the cause of the ruckus. Several sailors held torches and were arguing amongst each other in a panic.

"Quiet!" Davian ordered.

The men shrunk back, surprised that their leader had come out to speak to them.

"Lord Davian, we are sorry if we disturbed your repose," said one of the men.

"Never mind you that," the cigamian replied. "What is the problem here, boys?"

"We hate to trifle you with such matters, but one of the men, Johan, has gone missing," he answered.

Davian rolled his eyes. The last thing he needed was to babysit grown men, but in strange lands like this, one could never be too careful. "Where was he last?"

The sailor and the others led Davian to the area of thick forest where their comrade had last been seen clearing brush for the trail ahead. Davian flicked his robes open and pulled out his wand, setting it aglow to light his way in the dark wood.

He stepped over fat red vines and spiny palms and exotic ferns, casting his glance this way and that. One of the men suddenly cried out, nearly giving him a start.

"There he is! It's Johan!" one man cried out, pointing between some trees.

One hunched burly figure stood far off in the darkness alone, facing away from them.

"Sailor!" Davian ordered. "Speak your name."

There was only silence for several seconds as the shadowy man just stood in place, swaying back and forth slightly.

"What is your name, sailor? What are you doing there? I won't ask again," Davian threatened.

Everything was silent once again. Johan's shoulders and arms twitched eerily in the distance.

"Lord Davian-" began one of the men.

"Back away, boys!" Davian shouted.

The lone man turned around to face them and began to

shake violently. First his head, then his arms and legs began to spasm violently. Johan's body was changing dramatically in shape, quickly becoming unrecognizable. His skin and flesh looked flabby, almost melted and he bore a strange wide smile. His inhuman eyes twinkled in the moonlight and with a snarl, he lunged for the closest man.

Davian fired a blast of energy from his wand, but to his surprise, the twisted heap of a man was able to deflect the blast with one of his meaty hands. He'd have to try another approach. This time, Davian prepared a different spell. A pulsating black ball of cigam energy left his hands and flew towards the beast that Johan had become.

A tall man armed with a sword suddenly took a screaming thrust at the monster.

"I said to stay back!" Davian shouted angrily.

It was too late. The man struck with his sword, but when the sword connected with its body, the monster didn't appear harmed and in retaliation, it clamped onto the man's sword arm with its vile black teeth. At the same time, Davian's spell had struck it in its other hand, which tried to deflect the spell. The black light engulfed its misshapen paw and began to rush up towards the rest of its body. Any tissue touching the black light disintegrated. First, the skin crisped up and flaked away, then the muscle tissue smoldered and burnt into powder. It spread from the monster's jaws even, to the bitten man's arm, instantly liquefying his injured arm. He screamed in agony as the flesh on his arm melted as if it were in hot lava, and the spell soon worked its way up his shoulder.

Frustrated, Davian finished off the beast with another blast and then glared down at the dying man.

"Do you boys see why it is important to follow my instructions? When I say to stay back, you stay back," he growled. "Now I have to finish you before you infect the others."

The man shook his head madly and tried to clutch his melting arm with his good hand, which only caused his good fingers to begin to dissolve as well. "No! Please!"

"I'll make it quick and painless. It is better than dying like this, sailor," Davian replied almost sadly.

"Please! I-" Before he could say anymore, the man had been reduced to a pile of brown ashes.

"All right boys, stay together and let's get going. We've stayed long enough here. It is no longer safe."

It would take about an hour to get ready and it was still several hours until dawn. The men hadn't gotten to rest very much. While everyone began to pack up their belongings and gear and re-hitch the horses to their wagons, Davian felt something.

"Can it be?" he wondered. It felt like a burst of cigam from fairly close by. Several of them, in fact. There was no mistake. "Could there be another cigamian here, trying to get to my dragon?"

He smirked to himself. Perhaps it was the one that intended to face him. Maybe he'd even be something of a challenge.

"Come and face me," he dared.

CHAPTER THIRTY-FIVE: TRACING THE TRAIL

Sheriff Dingle had gotten back early to Jbug's house with many hours to spare before his noon deadline. Though it was still the wee hours of the morning, Rijo and his gang decided to use the sheriff's early arrival to get a head start on their search. They were packed up and headed out before daybreak. Dingle bade a silent farewell to his town of Nidum, unsure of whether he would return home safely.

Rogg, the tall thug with the scraggly brown hair, was leading the way. Evidently, he was the group's tracker.

"No man is better than Rogg at tracking," explained Rijo. "He's memorized the bloody footprints of the bastard who killed our boys, and he can seek it out along any trail. He can even tell you how long ago the track was made."

"That's amazing," Dingle replied hollowly, trying to be polite. He was more worried about other things of course, such as the safety of his hometown and himself.

They had headed straight for the main crossroads outside of town. Gree held a lamp over the ground and Rogg was poring over the dusty footprints in the cobbled circle. Dingle was skeptical that the man would be able to pick out the correct tracks amongst all the other prints that had accumulated since then, especially at night under lamplight. It had been far too long ago for there to be any evidence left.

The leader, Rijo, seemed to be paying attention to Dingle's take on the scene. "Have faith, Sheriff. He's the best. With Rogg on our team, there's no way we won't find the murderer."

Dingle nodded curtly and continued watching them work quietly.

"There's four of them," Rogg suddenly said aloud, surprising the sheriff.

"What do you mean?" asked Dingle. "You mean there were accomplices to the murder?"

Rogg rolled his eyes. "No, anyone with eyes can see that only the bastard's tracks leave from Jbug's house," he scoffed. "He was alone when he killed our boys. But somewhere along the way, he reconvened with three traveling companions to leave town."

"Who's he traveling with?"

Rogg gestured to the prints on the ground, but Dingle couldn't see anything but vague scuffs in the dirt. He had no idea how Rogg could make any sort of sense out of it.

"Judging from the size of the foot, the disproportionately wide shape, and the short gait, two of the three are dwarves," he explained, tracing the shape in the air above the prints. "The other set of prints are some other man I am unfamiliar with."

"That's incredible that you can tell so much from such faded footprints," Dingle admitted.

"You can learn a lot if you walk with your eyes open," Rogg smirked.

"You'd make a great detective," Dingle commented. "It's a shame not to have someone with your skills on the side of the law."

"Who asked for your two cents?" spat JJ.

Dingle shrugged. "Sorry, I didn't mean to offend. I was just thinking that a person with such rare ability could make a pretty penny working for the police force."

"If we want your pretty penny, we'll just take it from you, Sheriff," JJ concluded.

"Okay, I got it," Dingle responded. He decided the less he said, the better.

"We go this way," said Rogg finally, pointing south.

"All right, everyone! We'll avenge our boys!" declared Rijo.

The group whooped in concurrence and headed on with Dingle following them with distinctly less enthusiasm.

The trail ahead was pitch black beyond the yellow light of their lamps and strange animal noises whispered in the distance from either side of the trail. Dingle began to wonder if it was such a great idea to be starting the search at this time of day.

"Hey guys, I know we have no time to waste, but are you sure we should be traveling at dark?" Dingle asked.

"Afraid of the dark, Sheriff?" Gree joked.

"No, I mean, for one, it must be harder to track at night. Plus, it's more dangerous, with all the wild beasts out there hunting for food," he answered.

Rogg shot Dingle a look. "Don't question my methods, Sheriff. I can track any man at any time of day. Plus, it is we who are the hunters. Not the other way around. Don't forget it."

Dingle nodded and sighed. The group would never accept any of his suggestions. He followed along carefully, making sure not to trip on rocks or tree roots that were hard to see in the darkness.

They'd been traveling for a few hours when he felt eyes watching them. It was still just before daybreak, a prime time for untamed beasts to get their last meals before retiring for the day. Dingle looked around and saw what he was looking for. Several pairs of shining golden green eyes were gazing at them from the shrubs nearby them. Scratching noises came from the bushes as whatever they were would follow them along the trail.

"We got company, boys," Rijo stated, obviously having noticed the animal stalking them for a while too.

Everyone reached for their swords. Each of the six gang members carried deadly-looking blades, each with gleaming sharp edges and wickedly serrated sides. Only Dingle carried a simple short sword stamped with the town seal, which was standard fare for a police officer.

Realizing they'd been found out, at least a half dozen huge snakes slithered out of the shrubs. They were fatter than a person's thigh and each well over six feet long. The snakes' scales were shining black like obsidian, contrasting sharply with their bright green eyes.

"Man, not these," groaned Jar.

"What is it?" asked Dingle.

"Don't you know the beasts roaming outside your own

city?" asked Jar incredulously.

Dingle shifted uncomfortably at the accusation. "Sorry, I just don't travel out of Nidum after dark."

"Well, sheltered city-boy, these are some of the more dangerous animals that could be stalking you at night. Unlike most snakes, these serpents hunt in packs. They rip apart their prey and swallow the pieces whole. I've seen them swallow whole men before too."

Dingle thought he might be turning as green as the snakes' eyes, listening to Jar's description.

"They're also highly venomous—so don't get bit!" he explained.

Dingle gritted his teeth. Attacks from deadly poisonous animals that he could hardly even see? That was a perfect reason why no one should ever travel outside town at night. He didn't have any choice about it though. They had to fight.

Raij and Jar, the shorter stockier men, rushed forward with the swords. Belying their rotund figures, they were actually very fast and agile.

"We can't just back away from them?" Dingle asked aloud.

"Sheriff, grow a backbone!" Gree replied. "They've got a whiff of dinner. We fight to stay alive!" He rushed at the snakes with sword overhead, hollering madly.

Dingle's heart raced. Nidum was a relatively safe and peaceful place. He had never been in a truly life-threatening situation before. His hands clenched around the hilt of his short sword even harder. He'd never used his sword in real combat, just spars with Rangle or the other officers.

He saw Gree take a swipe at a serpent's head, but only grazed it, scraping off many scales. The reptile hissed shrilly in pain and recoiled backwards into the darkness. The leader, Rijo, was no coward either. He wove side to side, dodging venomous strikes form the creatures, lashing out with his own blade.

Dingle kept backing up nervously, trying to stay out of the line of danger, out of the serpents' range. A telltale hiss told him that his retreat was in vain. The sheriff spun around, holding the sword before himself in terror. One of the snakes has snuck up behind him and lunged in for the kill. Nearly stumbling over backwards, Dingle moved out of the way just in the nick of time, having the poison-filled fangs only just rip into the outer layer of his uniform rather than into his skin. He cried out and swung his sword blindly, connecting with the snake's neck and sending its head flying in a gross bloody mess.

Dingle panted for a few seconds to compose himself and steadied his shaking hands. He watched as the other men raged in battle against the rest of the reptilian threat. It was sure going to be a long night.

CHAPTER THIRTY-SIX: THE RESCUE

"We need a diversion," said Lorenz, starting out the plan.

"I can attack from-ah tha back with arrows," Unni suggested.

"And I can-ah hit tha group-ah midway in tha line," said Okin.

Danelo grimaced. "If Davian realizes that we're trying t'rescue meh brother, he'll kill 'im fer sure."

"Yeah, that's why I'm going to distract Davian," Lorenz said, surprising everyone.

"Yer sure?" asked Danelo, with a raised brow. "He's no man t'trifle with."

"Yes," Lorenz responded. He wasn't sure where his sudden bravery regarding Davian was coming from, but he just knew that he could do it. "It'll just be a quick distraction. I'm not going to fight him to the death or anything or crazy."

"Fine," agreed Danelo. "I'll lead us closer t'Davian's caravan. I'm sure he has many armed men with 'im. Be careful, everyone."

Keeping their own voices to a minimum, the four crept through the brush carefully and quietly as they could, getting closer to the distant sounds of men shouting and chopping through trees and brush to make way for wagons. After working their way through the vegetation, they got close enough to see the lamplight of the enemy caravan and hear the tromping of boots and clattering of wheels on the dirt. Luckily for them, the rustling sounds they made in the brush while sneaking up on the men were obscured by the noise of the dozens of men's talking and chopping and the rattling of their carts. Thanks to the racket, they were able to easily get close to the caravan.

Sitting forlornly in one of the lead carriages, Danilo suddenly stirred. He sensed his brother close by.

"I'm here, brother," Danelo told him silently.

Danilo just smiled to himself and kept quiet, not wanting to arouse any of the guards' suspicion.

At this point, the four heroes split up. Unni headed for

the end of the train, Okin headed for the middle, and Danelo and Lorenz aimed for the front. Lorenz needed a way to confuse the caravan. That required stopping the horses. The two men surmised that the lead wagon with all the guards stationed around it was probably either the cart with the prisoner Danilo or the leader Davian. Either way, that would work. Grinning, he pointed his wand to the trail before them, where the horses were clopping along. Vines and roots pulled up from the earth beneath them, grabbing and tangling up the horses' legs.

The horses stopped short and whinnied in fear.

"What's going on?" demanded one of the men, trying to calm one of the spooked horses.

Seeing that the train had stopped, Davian poked his head out of the carriage in frustration, trying to see what the commotion was about.

It was time for the next step. Lorenz aimed again and this time caused a front of dense clouds to form over the caravan and begin pouring rain in torrential buckets. The heavy drops fell so thick that the dirt on the trail was quickly turned to sticky mud and obscured everyone's vision.

Davian was alarmed. He knew it was the work of the one he'd sensed was near before. "Who is it?" he pondered. He scanned the tree line, trying to catch sight of the fool who dared to get in his way.

With chaos now consuming Davian's gang, the dwarves commenced their attack. Unni rained his arrows down on the end of the train, scattering men in a panic. Okin dashed into the fray with his axe, chopping up carts' wheels and axles to slow their progress, and then dove back into the bushes to hide.

The horse pulling Danilo's wagon lost its footing in the tangled vines and fell over, alarming the guards, who moved to upright the animal. Danilo took his chance. Still chained up in handcuffs, he jumped from the wagon and slammed ungracefully into the ground against his side and shoulder. Within moments, Danelo was at his side, helping him up and fleeing with him.

Now furious, Davian exited from his carriage and raised his hands with his wand in his right. Lorenz realized he needed to stop Davian from casting whatever spell he was doing, at least stopping him long enough to let the two pairs of brothers get away. An oldie but a goodie, Lorenz brought the vines by his feet up and made them try to twist over his legs. The trick worked. Davian angrily focused his attention to the annoying vegetation. He kicked at the weeds and blasted them with burning light from his wand, shriveling several of the vines.

In the light cast by his wand's spells, Lorenz caught his first real glimpse of the man. He could scarcely see him in the dark under his black robes in all the rain, but in those moments, Lorenz saw the face of evil. The lined face and greying hair of an older man did not hide the intensely blazing eyes and the snarled expression of a ruthless tyrant. Suddenly, in an instant that made Lorenz's blood run cold, Davian looked up, and uncannily stared straight into Lorenz's eyes. He'd seen him.

It was time to go. "Get out of here!" Lorenz projected into each of his friends' minds the way Thiek did to him all the time.

As they'd planned, they burst for the trees and they reunited a mile south of trail they'd been on previously. As Lorenz fled, he heard in his mind the menacing voice of his fated enemy.

"You'll pay for your defiance when we meet again."

"We'll see about that," Lorenz muttered to himself.

Back at the confusion of the caravan, Davian used his cigam to help repair some of the broken wagons in order to continue their journey. "Gather the men. Get them to stop acting like chickens with their heads cut off," he growled to the squad captain.

"Yes sir," he saluted. "I'm also sorry to report that the prisoner has escaped, Lord Davian."

"I know," Davian replied. "It's of no matter. We don't need him anymore. The dragon is very near now. We will find it."

NEXT TIME

Lorenz's adventure continues. They've survived yet another series of exhausting battles and rescued Danilo, but there is no time for rejoicing, as all their lives still hang in the balance. Davian won't rest until he's gotten his dragons and eliminated any threat to his rise to ultimate power.

Davian isn't the only one out for Lorenz's blood. Rijo and his gang, along with their hostage, Sheriff Dingle, are all on the hunt for our hero as well.

Meanwhile, Lorenz's life in his home world changes significantly. As he ages, his challenges become more complicated as he must take on unpleasant situations and learn to balance it all with his double life.

He has become something he could never have even dreamed of before and becomes torn when he must finally decide which world to remain in.

Follow along and prepare for the next installment of the story in:

Lorenz Traveling Diaries Part 3: Those from Underneath.